LIFE'S
DETOURS

LIFE'S DETOURS

Alexandra's Choices

BADIAA HIRESH

Copyright © 2021 Badiaa Hiresh.

All rights reserved. No part of this book may be used or reproduced by any means, graphic, electronic, or mechanical, including photocopying, recording, taping or by any information storage retrieval system without the written permission of the author except in the case of brief quotations embodied in critical articles and reviews.

This is a work of fiction. All of the characters, names, incidents, organizations, and dialogue in this novel are either the products of the author's imagination or are used fictitiously.

Archway Publishing books may be ordered through booksellers or by contacting:

Archway Publishing
1663 Liberty Drive
Bloomington, IN 47403
www.archwaypublishing.com
844-669-3957

Because of the dynamic nature of the Internet, any web addresses or links contained in this book may have changed since publication and may no longer be valid. The views expressed in this work are solely those of the author and do not necessarily reflect the views of the publisher, and the publisher hereby disclaims any responsibility for them.

Any people depicted in stock imagery provided by Getty Images are models, and such images are being used for illustrative purposes only. Certain stock imagery © Getty Images.

ISBN: 978-1-6657-0818-0 (sc)
ISBN: 978-1-6657-0819-7 (hc)
ISBN: 978-1-6657-0820-3 (e)

Library of Congress Control Number: 2021911905

Print information available on the last page.

Archway Publishing rev. date: 07/22/2021

To my angel.

To every parent: believe in your child's dream.
To every child: believe in yourself and your dream.
To every man: cherish the woman in your life.
To every woman: you are not alone. You are the master of your own destiny!

I dedicate this book to every woman, especially my daughters, Vanessa and Tiffany. I know I have pushed you to reach your goals, but it makes me proud to see you have reached further goals than I expected!

Dream big, be happy, and don't forget yourself along the path.

Wholeheartedly,
Your proud mom,
Badiaa

CHAPTER ONE

I don't know how to launch from here. I've reached a point where all I have is myself. I look around, and I see people smiling. I look at them, and I smile in return. Honestly, I don't know why I smile; all I know is that my smile got me here. My personality led me to today's outcome, and with no regrets, I am looking back, trying to understand.

This book tells many stories, but basically, it is the story of one woman. It is the "What if?" story that every woman tells herself. *What if I had taken the other route the day I stood at the crossroad and wondered which way to go?* The answer, of course, is uncertain.

I was a small-town girl born on December 6, 1964. I was born to a family of six children: four sons and two daughters, including myself. My father was a farmer, and his dream was to open his own farm. My mother was a beautiful lady, but more importantly, she had a beautiful soul. She was the one who kept the family together and the ties to the community connected. Mainly, she tried to build the dairy empire my dad always dreamed about.

The small town I belonged to was in the United Kingdom. It was called Farmville. The population was about sixty thousand, and it was well known for its products, greenery, and welcoming environment; additionally, it was by a seaport that connected the UK to the outside world.

I was the youngest of the family but the one with the biggest dream and the most guts. My dream was bigger than the small town I lived in, and when I looked at my parents and how hard they worked, I would tell myself, *No, not me—I will never end up a farmer.*

I used to look at my dad, who had white hair covering his head at the age of forty, when he came home late at night with barely any energy to speak, while my mom stayed up all night working hard to finish the dairy products she'd sell the next day.

Farmville was busy all the time, with businessmen coming in for seaport shipments. Most of the time, they came alone, but at times, they dragged their families along. Farmville had no hotels, so the citizens of the area built extra rooms to host the visitors for extra income. Most would have imagined a seaport area would grow quickly, but the citizens of Farmville insisted on maintaining its natural spirit. That was when my dreams started building up. I used to look at the visitors—their clothes, their hair, the money they spent when in town—and then at my parents and wonder why my parents, who were very hardworking, could not dream outside the box and seize these opportunities.

When I was in my early teens, while my brothers and sister were helping my father and mother, I would sit on the sidewalk of the seaport, watching the loading and unloading of the ships and the departures and arrivals, and with every departure, I would tell myself, *I will be on the next one.*

Schools were limited. We had six schools that worked double shifts to accommodate all the children. My parents were insistent on education. There were universities in the nearby cities, but most parents limited their children to primary and secondary school education only. Higher education was my first option out of Farmville.

When I was almost fifteen, my father had a car accident that left him with a physical disability that made my mother the sole worker in the house. She had two choices: reduce the farm's production, which would put the family in financial difficulty, or pull my two elder brothers and sister out of school to maintain the growth of the production and financial stability. She did the latter.

By that time, more strangers were visiting town. A businessman hired my sister as a nanny for his children, and soon after, he married her. The money received was a great support to the family. I begged my sister not to go, but unfortunately, she had no say in the matter. That worried me, especially after my younger brothers were pulled out of school. I knew that next it would be my turn, and then I could bid farewell to my dream of leaving Farmville. I was a selfish brat, thinking I was better than all my siblings, but in my heart, I had a dream, and in my mind, I had the will. I became more determined to succeed and prove myself.

I did not have the know-how, nor did I know what to expect, and the worst part was the financial difficulty we faced as a family. One night, at the dinner table, when we were discussing our situation, I recommended opening a small pub with music. Of course, my mom was dismissive, but I knew in my heart it would bring great income to the town. My father, who spoke less and less frequently, looked at me with a smile on his face and started crying. He knew my soul was bigger than Farmville, and more importantly, he knew I had a dream. I used to sit by the side of his bed at night and tell him weird stories. The stories were about a girl who left the comfort of her home to conquer the big world, and he knew the stories were about me and my dream.

One evening, I spoke to my mom and told her about my dream of continuing to higher education. Of course, she had no choice other than to forbid me from opening the subject, fearing I would keep on dreaming.

My dream was my only survival tool, so one day after school, I went to town and suggested my idea to a nearby home. They loved the idea and hired me to work as a waitress. One evening, as I was serving, a young man came in with his guitar. As he was playing among the crowd, I started humming and singing quietly. He grabbed me by the arm and made me sit by him. I started singing, and after that, I started entertaining every night. I was close to sixteen, with the attitude of a grown woman.

That night, I went home and told my mother I had gotten a night job as a waitress. She was not thrilled, but I told her I was staying in school and would be both supporting her financially and saving for my college education. It broke her heart, and my choice was against both my parents' will, but I told her I would not stop.

Day after day, more people came to my workplace. It was the town's only place of entertainment, and with my singing, more people started coming to town for vacation. Every night, after my shift, I would walk home alone. I used to go sit by the beach and dream about the ship that would take me to my own destiny. Was it wrong to dream? To me, the answer was no, but of course, to my family, it was against their way of thinking.

Shortly after, my parents, because we lived in a small town, heard about my singing. That night, when I got home, both my parents were up waiting. I opened the door, and they were sitting there. I looked beside them and saw that they had my clothes packed in a blanket. They said four words: "You have a choice." I knew what they were saying: I could either drop my work or leave the family home.

They were determined, so I had no choice: I said goodbye, I grabbed my clothes, and back to work I went, where the family hosted me.

In my heart, I felt a torn feeling, a deep wound, and a question: Why couldn't my parents accept me? But I couldn't blame them; they were not the type of family who could adapt to change. They were a Catholic family who believed that God gave us what we deserved. I was Catholic at heart, but in my mind, there was a call to dare to explore the blessings we were born to discover and the dreams we were on earth to pursue.

I knew that singing was not my dream, but I also knew that my voice was the blessing given to me to reach my dream. Although I was only sixteen, I used all my power to succeed.

During the day, I stayed in school. Education was my priority. In the evenings, my voice was getting higher and stronger, and more people were coming into town. Farmville was growing, as I was, and as much as that was an advantage, it made me more susceptible to harassment by drunk men as a single young woman alone.

I started to understand my parents' point of view, but nevertheless, I did not look back. The ocean became my mother and confidante. I missed my father's hugs, and I missed my mother's kisses and words of reassurance, but I found a safe haven in a treasure box filled with little notes and thoughts I used to write every time I sat by the ocean.

One night, after my performance, I was walking on the beach. I was too tired to even think, so I sat on a rock by the side of the ocean. Ships were loading and unloading. People were busy with their own things. I opened my treasure box and started browsing the past. Even at that young age, the box was far from empty; it held a bunch of papers I had written night after night, carrying my thoughts and feelings of long nights full of tears and emotions. I decided not to read them, but I could not throw them away. I put them in order and got myself a diary, which I used to keep my thoughts in order. Moreover, I promised myself I would write every night to make sure once I got my parents back one day, they would know they had been part of my every day, night, and moment.

That specific night was special, and it marked a change in the path of my life. Sometimes decisions parents made in a moment forced unforeseen fate to take charge, and that was what happened.

I was sitting on the rock by the beach, thinking about the next boat, with not a single sound other than the waves splashing on the rocks, and my heartbeat escalated with my thoughts. With droplets of water splattering on my feet and cheeks, I closed my eyes and dreamed of myself walking toward the next boat. Then I heard a noise—I heard footsteps. I looked around, but it was too dark to see;

no light was shining other than the starlight. So I closed my eyes again and tried to continue my dream, but I was interrupted by the voice of a man. I looked up, and he was standing there—a man in his early thirties. I looked at him, and he was familiar. He was a regular customer at the place where I sang nightly, and lately, he'd tried to get close to me.

It was only normal that when people saw someone often, they no longer considered the person a stranger, and additionally, I had a friendly character that made people feel comfortable talking to me and want to talk to me. That was how it all started.

The gentleman said, "Indeed, it is a precious view."

I looked at him, smiled, and said, "This rock has seated me since I was very young, and yes, it is precious, a precious view."

He said, "I meant you."

I looked at him. He was already seated beside me. I turned red, as it was the first direct compliment someone ever had given me.

"Do you mind?" he said while opening his bag and taking out two glasses and a bottle of wine. He poured the wine but never offered me the glass.

He started drinking and talking. "I have been watching you for a while. I came the first time to Farmville to escape the crowd of the city. I watched you singing. It was three months ago, and I left after that, leaving a piece of my heart behind me. I couldn't take my heart along. I traveled, and my thoughts were here, thinking about the magical presence you rained on us travelers and me particularly. Your voice fell on me like magic, and ever since, I could not focus outside Farmville. I started taking my car here weekly. Just knowing I would see you after the long drive was enough for me to make the journey. I used to follow you every evening and sit behind the tree far up, just watching you. I never dared to invade the beautiful private moments you obviously look forward to having, till this day."

I found myself drinking. It was my first glass of wine ever, and as time passed that evening, it was my first bottle. I was only seventeen, he was in his early thirties, and I fell for him. No words could have described my joy.

It was obvious he was well experienced, and he knew I was not. After a while, he stood, kissed my hand softly, and left, taking my heart along. After walking a few steps, he looked back and said, "I will see you tomorrow."

Tomorrow was a continuity, except he walked me to my rock and never left for a week. His name was Alex, and my name was Alexandra. I started seeing signs in our acquaintance, and I wished my mom were around so I could tell her how I felt, as it was my first crush, but sadly, my parents could not accept a dreamer. I hoped that one day I would sit with her, and we would read my diary together and restore all the lost time. The separation broke my heart. Why couldn't they see my dream and accept my odd soul? I knew they were a traditional Catholic family. I was too, but I was a dreamer, a flying soul. I was bigger than Farmville.

Alex and I were inseparable, and the gossip started in Farmville. It was the late 1970s and early '80s, and I was sure the news reached my parents and aggravated them more. I had no intention of getting married, and neither did Alex. I was just enjoying his company while falling in love. Our relationship got deeper, and I sank into emotions I had never experienced before; however, the relationship was purely platonic, despite the gossip.

Alex tried to get to know more about me from me, but I refused to discuss my personal life. He knew what he knew from what he heard, not from me, as I was ashamed to say that I had been rejected by my own family and, especially, that until I'd met him, my life had been pure, and my soul was not scratched.

I always knew that a girl without a father was like a bird without wings, with no protection and no status. I was a small-town girl with a dream, determined to succeed on her own with a strong will to reach her goal; I was bigger than that town and was waiting for the perfect time to debark and explore the big city.

Soon after, my feelings toward Alex, and his feelings toward me, started developing. The platonic love started evolving, and our weekends on the rock were cuddlier.

Was it wrong to fall in love? Why was I letting my emotions take over my destiny, knowing I would never settle for marriage? Was it the aching for fatherly love that made me fall for an older, wiser, and more experienced man, or was I truly in love? They were questions I had no answers to, nor was I ready to ask myself. I cared only about my happiness, nurturing my soul with the sweetness of Alex, the attention, and the emptiness he was filling. I knew he was not there to stay forever, because I was not ready to settle. My dream of the big city was always my priority, despite all the love he offered me.

The fall season started, and the skies were full of clouds, thunder, and rain. Sometimes I walked in the storm to sit alone by the beach, to feel the skies sharing my thoughts and the winds carrying my wishes. Other times, I couldn't; the storms were too strong. I would watch the ocean from afar from my window and try to hold my treasure box with my thoughts, fearing it would go with the flow of the water surging from the rain. But then I would remember that the hole it was saved in was as deep as my pain, and it protected my diary and my story.

The stormy weather prevented Alex from visiting every weekend, but the ties he had with me made him take the trip despite the weather, and he stayed longer. Missing each other made us long for each other and want each other more, and the platonic love transformed into heated nights. We agreed not to get fully involved, but it seemed the flames of the candles in the room, the fireplace, and the wine were stronger than our will, or mine at least.

One night, after my shift, the storm was bad, yet I insisted on going to the rock. Alex walked me, but as the rain was pouring, I got soaked in water and was cold, so he hugged me back to his room, where he put on the fireplace to keep me warm. I was shivering from the cold, and he started removing my wet layers of clothes in order to put them by the fire to dry. Layer after layer, I had nothing on. He placed pillows by the fireplace, where he seated me, and he covered me with a blanket and embraced me with his strong arms. With my head leaning on his shoulder, I hid my face against his neck, smelling him.

I started kissing him softly and rubbing my lips on his neck. I opened the doors of a passionate, endless time without thinking or worrying; I wanted his love. I wanted to feel his chest. I wanted him.

I did not realize what I had started. Being the gentleman he was, he had kept his clothes on. He put me down on the pillow and sat behind me, hugging me with his arms. We started drinking. I was still shivering, and I couldn't stop. I knew I was no longer cold; I knew my blood was boiling inside my veins. He moved slowly from behind me, added pillows for my support, went in front of me, and started massaging my feet. He asked me to close my eyes. I then felt his lips on my toes. I felt his hands moving up my legs. I did not know what to do. I had no experience, but obviously, his hands and lips knew the path toward ecstasy.

Shortly after, he removed his clothes. I felt his lips strolling upward from my toes, toward my stomach, and under the cover, I felt a heated storm. Then he stopped. I opened my eyes, and there he was, lying under the cover with me, staring at me.

Did time stop? I wished it would. Unfortunately, the heated storm was stronger than both our wills. He couldn't hold himself, while I did not know what to expect. I was feeling the time changing. We had drunk so much that I couldn't stop him.

"No, no, no," I said. I screamed and screamed, but time was faster than my words, and what happened could never be corrected. I cried like a baby and wished time had frozen earlier, but it was too late.

He went into a deep sleep with his arms surrounding me. *Where do I go from here? What will I do with myself if I get up and leave now?* Already I had become the talk of the town. I just stared at the skies, waiting for the sun to come up, and in the early hours of dawn, I sneaked out and went to my place, hoping what I feared would not happen.

The next morning, he woke up and came looking for me, but I was afraid to see him. So he left, going back to work. Week after week, he came back, driving in the middle of the storm. I avoided seeing him. I avoided talking to him. I hoped the damage would not be permanent, but my fearful thoughts were in place. A month after, I discovered I was pregnant. The world's heaviest load fell on me. *What should I do? Where do I go from here?*

I waited for him. The weekend came, and he never

showed up. The next weekend came, and he never showed up. My fear started growing, along with my belly, yet it was still in the beginning. I lost hope of his coming back.

One Friday, after my shift, I went to the rock, pleading for a solution. There I sat, writing and crying, when I felt his arms surround me. I jumped and cried in his arms, and he thought I was missing him.

He apologized for the night we'd spent together and what had resulted from it, but I kept weeping, and then I told him I was pregnant. He froze. He was scared but said not to worry. I smiled, but it turned out he wanted me to abort the baby. At that moment, I realized the weight of my mistake. I acknowledged the stupidity of love and asked him to leave.

Week after week, I waited for him to come back, hoping he would be rational, but unfortunately, my belly could not wait and gave me no choice but to collect my money, pack my clothes, dig a deep hole for my treasure box, and embark on the next boat to find my own destiny.

CHAPTER TWO

I tied my clothes in a bedsheet and snuck them out of my room. I hid them under the rock, and one night, after my shift, I knew it was time. I left with a wound in my heart and walked toward the rock. I sat there waiting for people to leave the deck. When everyone was gone, I grabbed my blanket and walked toward the unknown.

With small steps, I took the road, but with a giant heart, I faced my destiny. *Fear shall only hold me back*, I told myself. *We are all born with a mission and for a reason, and I may not know mine yet, but I will with time.* I reached the boat, bought my one-way ticket, and walked up the rail. Midway toward the end, I told myself, *No looking back.* Gravity was pulling me toward my will and destiny, while my heart was pulling me back to Farmville. I knew that pull came from fear of the unknown and the fact that I would be away from my parents. By leaving, I would be losing any chance of being close to them again. Like a tide, I was moving up with the wind, but the gravity to my hometown was calling me back. But this time, the gravity of my destiny was stronger, and I told myself, *I will turn around to face Farmville, but I will walk backward toward the boat. I am not afraid to say goodbye, because the farewell with my parents ended long before; it ended the day they packed my clothes.*

I reached the boat, turned around, and stood there waiting for the siren signal. Soon after, they pulled the rail out. Although I couldn't stop my tears, I started feeling strength fill my soul. *Those will be my last tears Farmville*, I told myself. *I will not feel sorry for myself. Instead, I will pull myself together, and with almighty power, I will move on.*

Indeed, I did. The smoke started rising, and I stood there waving goodbye to Farmville, to the city that had launched my dream. *Yes, I am a small-town girl, but I am determined to reach my destination in the Big Lady City.* That was what I called New York, from the pictures of voyagers I'd seen and the stories I'd heard. I wanted to reach her and build my castle around her.

Slowly, Farmville disappeared. The lights dimmed one after the other, until the only light left was the light of my room in my father's house. *Papa, I will never turn it off. I will come back to hug you and feel your tenderness. I truly wish I had your blessing, but in my heart, I know you wish me success.*

Morning sickness hit strong, and not having enough money to sleep in a room, I spent the nights sleeping on a mattress on the floor. I was told we needed four to six weeks to reach the Big Lady City, so I asked for a job on the ship. I was offered a room-cleaning position in return for food, only because the captain had seen me sitting on the rock day after day every time he came to Farmville. He asked me if I wanted to sing, but I had promised myself not to sing ever again. So against the lack of energy, morning sickness, and fatigue, I took on the job. I never would have thought that job would be a key to my future, through which I would meet businesspeople from the Big Lady City, but it was, and being one woman among few made me an additional target for those needing to talk and chat with the other gender.

The trip was long and tiring. My belly was showing, but I wasn't thinking about it yet. One night, as I was standing out on the deck, relaxing before going to sleep, a lady came to me. She was older, sophisticatedly dressed, and obviously from a well-established background. "Where is the father?" she asked.

I looked at her and said, "Is it obvious?"

"It takes one to know one. I have been there. I was your age, but I never had the courage to take the ride." Her words gave me strength and reassured me that I was not alone out there and, more importantly, was not a first.

I respected this lady a lot, and mostly, I respected that no questions were asked. We started meeting every night on the deck, in the middle of nowhere. She guided me through my pregnancy, and still, no questions were asked. But around that time, as we got close to the Big Lady City, I started thinking about the baby and the possible solutions.

One night, I was standing with the lady, and I opened up to her, telling her about my thoughts. I felt I was talking to my mother, and she was a great listener.

I told her, "I cannot raise the baby alone."

She smiled and said I was not alone. But still, in my dream and goals, I knew I could not offer the baby the life it deserved to have. I would have been condemning the baby to gossip and additional problems. Deep in my heart,

I wanted the best for the unborn, and I knew that with me, the baby could not have the best. Throughout the conversation, the lady begged me not to make any decisions till we reached a safe land. Additionally, she informed me that she owned a hotel and said I could stay with her till I found a job. This was a great beginning. She even offered me prenatal care with her gynecologist. It was a great comfort and provided something I was missing and worried about. I took her offer and promised her in return to choose the destiny of the baby with her.

We were informed that we would reach the safe land in a couple of days, and the excitement was obvious on my face. With it, I gained a great energy. The next morning, I woke up to the sound of the siren. I went up onto the deck, rushing to see the Big Lady standing there, holding the torch of liberty.

I could not describe my feelings, whether fear of the unknown or joy of reaching my destination safely, but I was happy.

A couple of days later, we reached land. I had my clothes wrapped and ready, but the main question was, how ready was I? A car was waiting for the generous lady. She waited for me, and off we went to her hotel. She offered me a room, as she had promised, and told me to get settled and rest and then meet her for dinner.

A young man joined us. He was my age, and she introduced him to me as her son. We sat, ate, and laughed, and I started wondering about her husband, but I never asked. When her son excused himself, she looked at me and said, "You remember what I said: you are not alone, even if the father does not exist."

I smiled and said, "I can never thank you enough."

But there the conversation started. She did not want to

know about the past but, rather, about my intentions for the future of the unborn. I asked her about the doctor. She had already arranged for me to see him the next morning and offered to join me.

The next morning, we went to the doctor. He checked me and told me the baby was healthy, and I was about seven weeks along. He asked me about the father, I said there wasn't one. Then I asked him about my options. He knew I was considering termination of the pregnancy, and directly, he moved the conversation toward giving the baby up for adoption. I looked at the lady, and she had tears in her eyes and said, "Allow me to interfere. The baby deserves a family and the life it was given. Don't condemn its future based on your past."

I was concerned about the future of the baby and the kind of life I could provide. The doctor said many families were not blessed with children and would love to adopt a healthy newborn. They both begged me not to decide now and, basically, not to go through with the termination. We went back home. In my heart, I did not want the termination, but I knew I could not be responsible for another soul.

Days went by, and the lady, one night at the dinner table, asked me about my interests. I told her about the only thing I always had known: I wanted to succeed in the Big Lady City. I was interested in opening a small restaurant and practicing what I knew best—the food business—and expanding. She looked at me, smiled, put a hand out, and said, "Will you accept me as a partner?" I shook her hand and wondered whether I was dreaming, but no, it was real. She was real. I had already found a partner to launch my dream. She gave me a couple of weeks to look around the hotel and decide on a location and needs. While I was doing my homework, I realized she was reassuring me and providing security in order to ease my decision toward the unborn.

Two weeks passed. It was time to hand in my business plan and was my last chance to make my decision about keeping or aborting the pregnancy. As we were having dinner, I informed her of my decision to keep the baby, but as for keeping it or considering adoption, I needed time. Her smile was wider than her face, and she said, "This is the perfect first step."

With prenatal care ongoing, I got busy with the opening of the coffee shop. Her son assisted me with the opening. We opened the shop and called it Alisa's Café. We started hosting hotel guests, and before we knew it, we started receiving walk-ins from the neighborhood. I got busy with the pregnancy and the coffee shop, and I forgot my social life. Mainly, I knew that any social life would present questions and answers about my belly. I hadn't finalized my decision regarding the baby, but deep in my heart, I wanted for the baby the perfect family.

A month later, the lady announced she was going to London and would be away for at least two months, and the hotel and coffee shop would be in our custody. Her son and I started building a good friendship. He was a great support on a personal level as well as on a professional level.

Business was great for both the hotel and the coffee shop; meanwhile, my belly was growing. I was getting very tired, and I needed a lot of rest, yet I kept working. The days went fast, and one day, as we were working, we were surprised by the lady's arrival. The businesses required long hours of hard work, and I started feeling ill. She got worried, and we made an appointment with the doctor. He put me on bed rest for three weeks and, after that, a maximum of four consecutive hours of work per day and a maximum of two shifts. The baby was her priority, because she felt I never assumed responsibility for myself or the baby; all I cared about was the success of the job.

Per the doctor's recommendations, I took it easy and changed my lifestyle under her close supervision. One day she stepped into my room as I was resting, to find me in tears. She sat by the bed and asked me one question: "Have you made up your mind?"

The answer had more tears than words: yes, I had. She had feared this moment. I told her I was considering giving the baby up for adoption. She cried and tried to talk me out of it.

I told her, "I cannot offer my baby what I lost. I need to heal myself from the loss of my family, and at this stage, I am very weak and young. I have no know-how for parenting, and the baby deserves a home and a family."

She promised to help me through, and in case I changed my mind, again, she offered her help.

This lady was a God-sent angel for me. I had no doubt she would offer support, but as well, I knew she would be taking on the load of the baby in addition to my load. I was in no situation to take on that load and preferred a better place and family for the unborn.

I started thinking about my situation seriously. I knew a day would come when I would regret giving the baby up for adoption, but as well, I knew that a baby needed a father, a mother, and a secure home. I never knew where I would be tomorrow. All I knew was that my loyalty was to this lady who had opened her heart, home, and arms for me. I had to make a decision for the future and make sure I secured for the baby a family. So I started looking and inquiring, till one day, the lady came to me and told me she had found a family for the baby. They were ready and willing to adopt. I stopped her with a sudden word, and she looked at me, thinking I'd changed my mind. I told her no, I had not, but I wanted her to be the contact and do the proper paperwork, and I did not want to know anything about it. If I was to move on with my life, the baby needed to too, and it would be best for the baby to have a fully private and new start in which it was loved and wanted.

The decision might have seemed selfish, but I believed it was in the baby's best interest. I knew I should have been responsible for my actions, should have thought about the outcome of a passionate night, and might regret forever the decision and think about it every night for the rest of my life. But I was not running away from my duties; instead, I was taking charge of my life and giving the best to my unborn baby.

The day I decided to move on with the pregnancy was the day I accepted my responsibility. I was too young to raise a child, and the decision was for the best of both of us. I only hoped the baby would forgive me one day, and I hoped for forgiveness from above.

Months rolled by as she tried to choose the perfect family, until one day, the lady came to me with a surprise: she said she'd found the perfect family. I refused to know the details or the family, and I entrusted her with the choice. I thought someone who offered all she had must have been trustworthy with her decision, so I agreed. I signed papers for her to be in charge, but I requested that I buy the baby a necklace. We went to the market, and I chose a heart necklace. Inside it, I imprinted, "Love you forever."

I got close to my due date. The lady was still hoping I would change my mind, but I reaffirmed to her I was not. The day came. I started feeling the birth cramps. We went to the hospital, and I had a beautiful and healthy baby girl.

They asked me about the name, and my only request was to name her Alisa and to ensure the baby would keep her name. I held the baby in my arms, whispered all my love for her, and gave her away.

Where are you going, my child? I prefer not knowing, because I am sure you will be in better hands. You will be in my thoughts and prayers every night, but I cannot offer more.

A couple of days after, I checked out of the hospital and went home to start my own life. That phase was difficult because I missed the smell of my baby, yet I couldn't go back on my decision, knowing she would be in a better place.

I knew nothing about Alisa after that day at the hospital. I tried to keep myself busy and forget that phase of my life.

One might have thought of me as heartless, careless, and selfish, and that was what I thought of myself. But I believed I'd done what was best for myself and the baby.

With those thoughts, I moved on. I got back in shape and joined a club of young expats. We met every week to chat and plan different activities. *Hey, future, are you ready for me? Because I surely am ready. No regrets, no remorse, and surely no more tears.*

CHAPTER

THREE

The club of young expats was important and beneficial to me. I expanded my social network and met people from different backgrounds. Alisa's Café was booming, and the lady was happy. One night, as we were sitting and relaxing after work, she suggested I continue my education. The lady's recommendations were parental, and I was never able to understand her love toward me. Was it a coincidence that all heaven's doors opened through her, or was she in fact the most decent person I'd ever encountered? I believed I was blessed to have met her.

I told her I would like to take night courses in international cuisine. She loved the idea, and she took on the responsibility of finding me the right school. Within a week, she found me a school. I had classes two nights a week, which was perfect for me. I was excited; the courses would take twelve months, and I could practice at Alisa's Café.

Meanwhile, I met a young lady named Georgia, and we became friends. Georgia was from Germany, she was my age, and we met at the club. Georgia had moved to New York to continue her education; she was studying fashion design. Georgia was outgoing and enjoyed nightlife, which was one thing we did not share, especially because I had to keep up with my work and had my cuisine courses twice a week. Additionally, the lady did not approve of her personality and was concerned about her lifestyle. I tried to reassure her that I was safe, but as any parent would have, she got involved in my personal life, and I let her be. I'd deceived my own parents once, and I would not deceive the new parent God had sent me. So I balanced my relationship with Georgia in a way that I kept her friendship and did not upset the lady.

When people came from different backgrounds, it was difficult to mingle, accept others, and fit in. Georgia came from a well-established background. Everything had been organized for her before she moved, she could afford not to work, and she had enough money to spare and survive. Her character was not flexible, and she liked for things to happen her way and when she asked, yet she was a wonderful person and a good friend. She was someone who added laughter to her surroundings, which was a positive added value I needed in my day-to-day life. As for me, I was the rebel of my family, came from a small town in the United Kingdom, had family issues, and had a personal dilemma; nevertheless, I had learned that if you wanted to see your dreams happen, you needed to work hard, be strong, be fearless, and remain positive. That was how my social life started.

I introduced Georgia to Andrew, the lady's son, and together we created a friendly, supportive circle. Among the three of us, Andrew was the only one who had never been outside New York. His main interest was dancing, but his mother did not support his choice, so he danced secretly. He invited me once to watch his performance in the secret group he belonged to and begged me to convince his mother to let him be and accept his choice. I promised to talk to his mother in due time, because he felt she trusted my judgment and thought highly of me. I was to her the daughter she'd always dreamed of having. I respected Andrew a lot, and I respected the fact that he kept my life private.

The three of us started going out weekly together. The evening was of great interest to both Georgia and Andrew; he would dance, and she would drink and mingle with different people. My job was to keep an eye on both of them. I had no interest in meeting people; my focus was my priority. Although many tried to get close to me and get to know me, I told everyone I was engaged. I enjoyed my outings, but I took advantage of them to increase my network and introduce Alisa's Café, which brought more people to our hotel and café.

Soon after, the lady decided to expand the hotel by building an extension outside and creating more opportunities for me. My cooking classes were interesting, and I started taking the lead in the cuisine. The lady announced to me that the extension would be ready in a couple of months. We needed a bigger kitchen service, because in her vision, she believed the venue would attract wedding events. The lady was right on that point; within a month, we started receiving bookings that required lots of preparations. This step gave me more determination to succeed in my cuisine classes. The owner of the school was fond of my creativity and offered me a scholarship for the upcoming summer in one of the big cuisine courses. Although it would mean three weeks away from Alisa's Café, the lady believed it would be beneficial to me on a personal level and to the café at the same time. The scholarship was at one of the big hotels in New York, under the supervision of some of the biggest chefs, who were coming from all over Europe and the States, and it was fifteen minutes by metro from our hotel. I was worried about the load of work I was leaving behind, but the lady reassured me that all would be under her control.

The months passed quickly, and it was time to start my scholarship training. The lady called me one day to her office to inform me that she would have to travel. I asked her whether I should drop the scholarship, but she insisted on my accepting it and keeping Andrew in charge. It was a good time to discuss Andrew's passion for dance, so I opened the subject, and to my surprise, she knew all about it. In her mind, dancing would not secure a future for Andrew, and she needed him at the hotel; additionally, she had worked hard to build her throne. However, she didn't mind having him follow his dream now, especially with me there to take over the duties. I felt more responsibility toward her and more love and trust coming my way. I asked her to come watch him perform, because I believed he was talented, and she promised to do so after her trip. I never knew why she traveled, but I'd learned with her not to ask. She was a self-made woman who gave more than she took and was a great leader. She was my idol and role model; she was what I dreamed of becoming one day. I never worried about paying her back, because what she had offered me was far beyond being paid back.

One night, as we were out while the lady was traveling, I informed Andrew about my discussion with his mom. He was thrilled and gave me a big hug. I made him promise me he would always remain in support of his mom. He agreed with me, and we discussed her hard work. He told me that he felt I was her focus more than he was, yet he would never fail her.

During that evening, a new girl approached me. She was African. We spent the evening chatting, and we built a connection. Her name was Angela, and she was an exchange student at the University of New York. She felt lonely but determined to succeed. She was majoring in political science. Her parents back in Africa had great hopes for her and her degree, but it was not her dream. Back then, parents had great influence on their kids, and mostly, they decided their future. Angela was quiet, well structured, and smart, with excellent communication skills, which explained the choice of her parents, especially as she was an only child. Her dad was in politics, and he wanted her to follow in his footsteps. Angela's passion was toward legal studies, and that was the minor she was pursuing.

I knew the lady would approve of our friendship because Angela was a determined girl. Angela had a great voice, and she had a passion for singing, which reminded me of my old lost days, yet I never revealed to her my past. I introduced Angela to Georgia and Andrew, and together our circle became bigger. My scholarship courses were about to begin. Andrew promised to take good care of the hotel and café, Georgia kept busy with her own life, and Angela was looking for extra income next to her studies. I offered a singing job for her at the café. She accepted it with lots of joy, so we started entertaining the guests every weekend. The idea was received positively by the guests, and the café was booked nonstop. I wanted to surprise the lady and show her that her trust was in place.

Indeed, upon her return, she was thrilled to see the bookings and atmosphere, and mainly, she loved Angela's character. It was time to fulfill a promise, and that promise was toward Andrew. He had a big performance coming, and he was hoping to receive the consent of his mom. I spoke to her, she agreed to attend, and we both went to the performance.

As we were watching, I looked at her, and she had tears in her eyes. Without looking at me, she said, "He does remind me a lot of his dad." It was the first time she'd mentioned his dad. It was emotional, and her mentioning his dad brought memories back to me. Where were my parents? How come they'd never understood my character and accepted my dream? It was a question that never escaped my mind.

The performance ended, and it was a great success. Andrew was happy with his mom's attendance. She gave him a bouquet of flowers and a big hug, congratulating him, and we left. After the performance, the lady and I went for a drink. It was the first time we'd sat and chatted outside the hotel. We had a drink, and she opened up to me. For the first time, she told me about the father. It seemed everyone had a story that became the pillar of his or her future.

Andrew knew nothing about his dad, because his dad wanted nothing to do with Andrew. Andrew had come into the world against his dad's will. The father was a dancer, passionate about the dance floor and selfish. He had no intention of having a serious relationship or taking on himself any responsibilities toward the lady or the baby. Andrew's dad owned the hotel, and the lady was the manager. They fell in love, but obviously, he had no commitment toward his business. His main concern was the dance floor, and his passion was limited to himself and his success above anything. The lady loved him way more than he loved her, and she had more care toward the business than he did. The father joined a big dancing team that toured the world and kept going around, leaving everything behind. If not for the lady, the hotel would have vanished a long time ago. When the lady got pregnant, Andrew's father wanted to terminate the pregnancy. The lady wanted a family and a commitment, but her plan stood in the way of the father's dream. Therefore, he took the easy way out. He wrote the hotel into the lady's name, and that was where its name came from, Lady's Hotel. He dropped everything to follow his passion. Additionally, he requested that his fatherhood remain anonymous to the child. That was why Andrew knew nothing about his dad, although he inquired a lot. That was where Andrew's passion toward dance came from. Andrew showed passion toward dance throughout his childhood, and Lady knew that, but she feared losing Andrew as well; therefore, she never encouraged him to pursue his passion or allowed herself to accept it. Lady was still in love with the father and felt she could never accept another man in her life. She locked herself within her memory and dedicated her life to the success of the hotel. I guessed that was where her strength came from. There was a story behind every closed door. When Lady got pregnant, her parents rejected her and refused any contact with her. That explained a lot, including her support to me. It explained her question to me when we first met on the deck of the boat.

Then she said, "Enough about me. Update me on your studies."

"My scholarship courses were very exciting, and I proved myself among the big chefs. They even offered me a full-time job in the hotel."

She froze. "And your decision?"

I told her not to worry. "My answer to them was 'I have a great job and a great partner, and no money in the world will outstand what I have.'"

Lady was pleased with my success and congratulated me, but I wanted her to know I meant what I said. I told her, "You will never understand what you have offered me, from love to care to guidance. My loyalty toward you goes beyond my respect to you. You fulfilled my dream to succeed in the big world. You were my mother and my friend. You accepted me when my parents rejected me. I am with you to stay, to fulfill my dream and yours. And this is only the beginning of my dream. I know deep in your heart, you were not happy with me letting go of my baby, Alisa, but life is a journey, and both of us, Alisa and I, have our own. I did what I believed was best for both of us. You are my godmother, my savior, and as for Alisa, I am sure you placed her in a good home where she is loved and cherished."

Lady asked me whether I wanted to have news about Alisa, and my answer was no. I said, "It is better for her that I don't." She respected my wish and said no more. Later, I wrote a letter to my daughter:

> Dear Alisa, dearest daughter of mine,
>
> I hope you forgive me. Every night before I sleep, I hug the blanket that wrapped you in the hospital. I kiss it and sing you a lullaby good night that I learned especially for you. By now, you are about one year old. You probably said your first word. *Mommy*, I hope it was. It breaks my heart that you are not saying it to me. But I know you were

placed in a loving and caring home. I promise you I will never forget you, and I hope you will understand that my love for you is greater than any love I will ever share.

You will always be in my heart. I still remember your voice and your smell, and every night when I hug your blanket, it is you I am hugging. One day, probably, our paths will cross; meanwhile, you have my prayers, love, and thoughts. Love you eternally, my child.

Sadly, Alisa would never hear those words or read my note, because my wish was for her not to be informed about my identity. I would never forgive myself for what I had done, but it was the best I could offer. Life was situational, the choices we made were conditional, and what I chose was based on my situation.

I looked at Lady and said, "Do you think I am selfish? Do I remind you of Andrew's father?"

She said, "No. I wish we could know at times the outcomes of our decisions, but you did what was best for you and Alisa. Alisa is in good hands."

With those words, we ended the evening. We took a cab, hugged, and both went back to reality.

CHAPTER FOUR

Your secret is safe with me, dear lady, I thought. *Your empire is in good hands.* Indeed, with her sharing the secret of her life with me, I felt more dedicated to her than I ever had. *In life, we meet many people, but only few mark their prints in our soul.*

With time, the memory of my parents faded away—not out of anger but, rather, out of the love offered to me by Lady, who became my family away from home. I wondered whether my daughter would ever need my love if she found such love.

My professional life became more involved in the hotel and Alisa's Café, and my social life was ongoing with Angela, Georgia, and Andrew. We all had great commitments, but the nightlife was taking over our minds. Although my dedication was toward my work, slowly, I started enjoying the loud nights. We all agreed that one night per week was ours, with Lady's consent. We would start at the expat club and then switch to dancing. Around that time, New York started booming with different clubs. We were all young, beautiful, and full of life. I knew I had changed, as I had started enjoying the nightlife; nevertheless, I'd decided I would never allow a man in my life.

Life was smooth, tiring, and fun. It was the month of June, and a big day was coming our way: the Fourth of July, Independence Day. The hotel was booked with visitors from outside New York. Alisa's Café was as well. All food areas in town agreed to stop serving by eleven in the evening for everyone to take part in the midnight event. So we did, and as we wrapped a great, successful evening at the hotel and café, we all walked onto the pier to attend the midnight show. Drinks were served in booths by the pier, and the skies were sparkling with fireworks and loud noise. People were singing and dancing in the streets. I looked around, and I was alone. I guessed each swayed his or her own way. I stood there with my beer, looking up to the skies. Then I heard a voice say, "Aren't they beautiful?"

"Indeed," I said. "I just wish I could watch silently; my ears hurt."

He put down his beer and covered my ears with his hands. At that moment, I did not want to see the fireworks anymore. I closed my eyes and felt the sparkles in my heart. I wished the moment were a dream, because I had made a promise to myself that no men would access my personal life. His hands and his gesture were something I was longing for. I had forgotten the feeling of being touched by a gentleman.

I turned around in a brusque way, and he removed his hands, looked at me, and apologized. "Obviously, it wasn't the right move," he said, "but looking at you enjoying the fireworks, you looked like a dreamer, and I only wanted you to enjoy the moment. Can we start all over again? I am Robert."

"Alexandra," I said while I turned red.

"Would you like to take a walk on the beach?"

I nodded silently. So we walked on the sidewalk till we found an opening to the sandy area, and he bent down to remove his shoes. I was waiting for him to finish, and he looked up at me, grabbed the bottom of my leg, and then removed my sandals one after the other. I smiled. He held the shoes in his hand, stood up, and grabbed my hand to cross to the sandy area. All I could think was *Why are you so sweet?*

We walked toward the ocean, and he asked me whether I preferred to sit or walk. Of course, I wanted to sit to re-create an old memory. We sat, and he started telling me about himself. He worked as a captain for international flights, was twenty-eight, and traveled frequently. The first thing he did when he landed was come to the pier and walk by the ocean.

Usually, when someone introduced himself, the expectation was to do the same, so I told him, "I am a co-owner of Alisa's Café, I am currently finishing my chef studies, and I am the manager of Lady's Hotel."

"But your accent says you are not American," he said.

"No, I am British, coming from a small town in the UK, Farmville."

He started to ask a question, but I interrupted and said, "That is all I have to say about myself." I was not ready to share my story—nor I would ever be, in my mind—and respectfully, he asked no more.

He went on, telling me about his trips. Obviously, he was a dreamer, a mind I understood. We started laughing and talking, and he acted like a gentleman. Then I asked to leave, so we stood, and he walked me home to the hotel and left me at the gate. I went inside with my heart beating fast. Lady was waiting for me, and I ran to her and hugged her tightly. She smiled, we sat, and I told her all about my evening.

"You have his number? Did you exchange numbers?" she asked.

"No, I was not ready," I said. "I do not want any man in my life."

She let me be, and I went to bed. Of course, I could not sleep; instead, I sat in bed all night, looking up to the sky, gazing at the stars, and wondering about my life. *I am young, beautiful, and full of life. At what phase did I decide not to have a life anymore? Was it the time I was left pregnant? But even then, I had no intention of marrying. Or was it out of loyalty to Alisa, my daughter?* I did not have the answers, but the decision was clear to me: *No man shall ever access the firewall of my life.*

As the sun rose, I went down to the kitchen and started baking. Minutes after, I heard Lady say, "You couldn't sleep as well? Fix us coffee, and join me."

I knew deep in my heart that yesterday's discussion was not over; she'd just let me be for the night. I took the coffee and met her in our corner.

"You cannot make my mistake," she said. "Life does not stop at any station. Life goes on, and you have the right to live, dream, and be happy. Don't make the mistakes I did."

"Your words are so right," I said, but I still did not figure out at what point I'd dropped the will of taking care of myself. Had it been disobeying my parents, going the extent with a man I once loved, or letting go of my Alisa? They were questions I asked myself daily, but all I could come up with was what I'd promised myself: no man in my life.

"Alexandra, my dear," she said, "you are a parent now, regardless of the choice you have made regarding Alisa. The way your parents reacted toward you, a child dreamer, was their choice and not your fault. I am talking now as an experienced woman, someone who went through a similar situation, and a mother. I cannot answer for your parents, but I can assure you that being a dreamer is not a mistake. The world, without dreamers, would stop evolving. I can tell you one thing: never stop dreaming. You are what you make of every situation, and you are a successful dreamer. As for what happened with Alisa's father, with the few details I have, I can tell you that men in our life are a stage, not life itself, especially with women like us: well determined and strong enough to survive without them. As for Alisa, you were smart enough and strong enough to give her a family, something you could not offer her, and it's a strength I never had. She is in great hands. Anytime you are ready, I will give you details."

I stopped her there. "No, it's good enough for me to know she is happy."

"You entrusted me with her well-being, and she is in great hands. You have the right to be happy, and you deserve to be happy, so never lose that opportunity."

Lady's words were soothing, comforting, and from the heart. I thanked God every day for sending her my way. I didn't know where I would have been without her. She was my guardian angel, and I was blessed to have her in my life.

Back to the kitchen I went, not convinced to allow a man into my life but at least convinced I had the right to be happy. That day was different. I was baking without a written recipe. My heart was creating new recipes and new designs. All that was on the menu that day was the chef's specialty. Lady was shocked, but her trust in me was far beyond my trust in myself.

Usually, the day after the Fourth of July was slow everywhere, but Alisa's Café was booked for lunch. Lady came to me, saying she'd informed everyone about the change of menu, and everyone was thrilled to try new flavors. I took charge of the kitchen, and because of the new menu, I could not be out on the floor. Orders were coming nonstop, and there was a huge order for everything on the menu, with a special request to meet the chef. Lady came to me, saying, "You are wanted outside."

I said I couldn't, but she answered, "The customer will wait till the end." We both assumed it was a chef from my school.

I finished and went out, and to my surprise, it was Robert. As I got near his table, he had the table set for two, with a bottle of wine ready. "If you thought you got rid of me yesterday, you were wrong. I've sampled a bite from every plate, and I will be here for a long while."

I smiled and said, "Where is your companion?"

"Standing in front of me."

Lady came, removed my apron, pulled out the seat for me, and said, "Enjoy."

We sat there for hours, everyone left, and the conversation never ended. I excused myself to shower, and then we left. Robert joined me at the expat club, and we ended the evening on the beach. In the club, I introduced Robert to Angela and Georgia, and we invited them to come along, but Angela had tests the next day, and Georgia was going out with a group of people we'd never met.

Robert had the same impressions Lady had about the girls: full trust in Angela but reservation toward Georgia. I told him that was the same reaction Lady had, and he said, "You are mature enough to know how much to offer."

I'd heard those words before, but I liked that he did not impose an opinion over me. As we were walking on the beach, Robert told me he hadn't stopped thinking about me since the minute he left me. He was amazed with my character, and after tasting the food, he said he wouldn't want to eat elsewhere ever again.

Another determined man in my life. Why don't they go easy and take time to express their feelings? Don't they know this freaks out the woman? Don't they like to get to know the other person first? Is it age that makes them want to rush things?

He spoke as if reading my mind. "I know what I want when I see it, and the moment I closed your ears with my hands, I felt your heart and knew you were the woman of my dreams."

"Too direct and too fast," I said. "I prefer to take my time in getting to know people." But in my heart, I knew that was not true. "I believe that time will define us."

He said, "I am traveling tomorrow, going to France. You will have enough time to analyze our situation, but I will be back—and back for you."

Although I had known Robert for only two days, it felt longer, and knowing I would miss him, I believed I needed the space because of his rushed character and to avoid my telling him off.

We spent the evening walking on the beach, watching the stars, giving them names, and telling the stories of each star. It was obvious Robert was a romantic gentleman from the stories he told. I tried to avoid the romantic side in mine, but I was a romantic dreamer, and Robert brought out that side of me again.

Dreamers were passionate about life; they loved quickly, didn't fear the unknown, admired a challenge, trusted quickly, and embarked on journeys without plans. We both shared the same character, which probably was what had brought us together, in addition to our loving the feeling of the sand under our bare feet and the sound of the waves during silence.

As Robert shared his feelings and intentions out loud, I shared my thoughts silently, and knowing him so far, he could read my mind and feel my heartbeat. The night was coming to an end; despite our will to stay, we had to end it and walk back home to the hotel. Robert remained a gentleman; he did not even try to hold my hand, although I wanted to hold him tightly and thank him for the beautiful time. We reached the hotel; I wished him a safe flight; and as I was going in, I stopped at the table where we'd had lunch, a table for two, carrying new memories, waiting for our next meeting.

Robert left, and I went inside. I saw Lady waiting for me with sadness surrounding her. I asked her what was wrong, and she said she'd received a call from the hospital; Georgia had had an accident. The driver was waiting for us, and we took off to the hospital.

"How serious?" I asked.

She had no news, other than she had been called for being the person to contact in case of emergency. We were both in tears, fearing the unknown. We reached the hospital, went to ask about her, and were asked to sit in the waiting room till the doctors came out. We sat there, both thinking silently about the last time we had been there. I wrote a letter:

> Dearest Alisa, daughter of mine,
>
> I am here today in the hospital where I gave you away. I am here because a dear friend of mine had an accident, but all I can think of is you. You must be two by now. You are surely running in the house of your new family and filling their home with life and giggles. I am sure you are talking by now, and you are ready to get rid of your diapers. I don't know what you do before sleeping, but I know that I hold your hand every night to sleep. I tell you stories and hope you have a favorite one. I hold your hand, and we sit together on the rocking chair, singing your favorite lullaby. I imagine your beautiful smile. I know that no matter the distance, you should hear my words, as I feel your breath. I still have your blanket; your smell shadows me day in and day out. I may not have been the mother you expected, but you are the daughter every mother would dream of. So long, my daughter, and let life decide.

As I had before, I gave the letter to Lady, and she sealed it and did not read it. "Do you want to know about Alisa?" she asked.

I said no. I rested my head on her shoulder with tears. "Will she ever forgive me?" I said.

"Children are born with the power to love and not to judge," she said.

Then the doctor came out. "We contacted Georgia's parents in Germany. She had an accident on a motorcycle, and she is in critical condition. She needs our prayers. Go home now; we will contact you in case of any changes. Come back in the morning."

Off we went home with prayers in our hearts.

CHAPTER FIVE

Georgia's accident came as a shock, and not knowing any details about the accident scared me. For the time being, all I wanted was for her to wake up. I could not sleep; if I closed my eyes, I would see her smile, remember my times with her, and remember Lady's fear about her lifestyle, as well as Robert's. I prayed, *Please, God, do not take her away, and let her learn a lesson.*

I wondered how her parents had reacted to the call they'd received, and I started thinking about my own parents and asking, "What if?" but I guessed I was far beyond where Georgia was. I spent the night anxious, worried, and disturbed, and Lady did as well. I expected to hear her say at any minute, "I told you so. I always knew she would get herself in trouble. That is why I've been protecting you." But Lady let me understand her fear through her silence rather than her words, especially that we had no details ever about the circumstances of the accident or the outcomes.

With the first rays of sunrise, we were ready to go to the hospital. Georgia's parents were expected to arrive in the afternoon. The hospital staff and authorities would not allow us in her room, and the police were there investigating. They asked to speak to her close friends, and there we were. They asked questions about her lifestyle, friends' names, alcohol habits, and drugs. We were possessed by panic, especially that her condition was still unknown. Although Georgia's lifestyle was wild, the extent we knew was limited. We never ended an evening together; she was a wild drinker in terms of mixing alcohol intake, and additionally, she never feared strangers. I knew the police presence meant that someone was hurt, but why was no one giving us information about her condition or allowing us to see her? When Lady and I had a minute together, Lady asked me to limit my answers to the questions and never volunteer information they were not asking for. Nurses and police were going in and out of her room, meaning Georgia was still alive, and that was comforting.

A while after, the doctor we had seen on day one passed by. Lady followed him, and finally, we got some information. He said Georgia was awake. "Physically, she needs surgery, but now she is alert."

It was a good answer but not a reassuring one. "Now she is alert" meant that last night, she had not been. *Whatever happens, dear Georgia, please stay strong.*

Lady wanted to see her to advise her and see whether she needed a lawyer. She begged the doctors, saying her parents were still abroad, and she needed a loving hand to hold hers, as she was young and in a strange country. The doctors promised to try with the police, and finally, they said one of us could visit for ten minutes.

As a mom would have, and a rational adult, Lady

recommended she go in. Deep down, I was not ready to see the pain Georgia was going through without being prepared. The only time I had visited a hospital was to give birth. I guessed it was selfish, but I was afraid. Clearly, her situation was critical, and there were many unanswered questions. I was hoping to have some answers before Georgia's parents get there. It would be awkward not to have answers and, worse, not to know the facts. Lady was called in. She looked at me, and her eyes said, "God be with us." Meanwhile, I sat out there alone.

Luckily, Andrew and Angela came. They sat near me, and all of us waited together. They'd read the note we'd left them at the hotel. They did not ask questions. Like us, they only wanted answers. Our friendship with Georgia and each other was precious, deep, and rational. We all supported each other and accepted our differences, but we all knew Georgia was the wild and odd one. Her lifestyle was unrestricted, and she was racing with daylight to do it all. Her lifestyle was daring and was a message stating, "I decide on my own." We all loved Georgia and enjoyed her company, but we all feared her guts.

Soon after, Lady came out. She was pale and in tears. I knew directly it was ugly. Lady recommended we go down to the cafeteria. We sat there, and shortly after, Lady calmed down and relayed what she had seen.

"Georgia is alive and will make it, but the doctors don't know yet how. She can talk, but her fear is standing in the way. She wrote her words, asking about her parents. She's worried about their reaction. I guess she is in trouble. She was not alone on the motorcycle; the driver passed away directly. They were speeding, and they were drinking.

"Georgia's physical condition is better now, as it is stable, but her emotional condition is very worrisome.

They are still running more tests to figure out whether her silence is psychological or medical, and same for her mobility. The parents will need our support. I urge you to stay, but I cannot force you. And additionally, be strong. Beautiful Georgia is kind of disfigured, and she needs us in person to hold her hand and be there for her. Friendship is not about outings and fun times only; it's also about proving our support when need be."

Deep down, I knew there was a secret lying in that room with Georgia, and being the first friend she'd ever had in the States, I knew that I needed to be strong for her and that she needed me near. Nonetheless, at that point in her recovery, all I could do was let her know I was around.

We stayed in the hospital that afternoon till her parents arrived. The father spoke English, while the mother understood more than she spoke. Both had more tears and anger to share than words, which was expected. The mother kept saying, "Georgia," repeatedly. The dilemma of not knowing the facts, the reasons behind the accident, and the outcomes made their trip more dramatic. Upon their arrival to the hospital, they were directed to the area where we were sitting. The first moments were tough. Then the police called them in to inform them about the facts, and then they left the police area to go see Georgia. They went into the room, and a minute after, the father came out, banging his head on the wall and crying, while the mother stayed inside. The father could not see Georgia the way she was. Was she in such a bad situation physically, or was the father too emotional? I was so worried about Georgia. I just wanted to go in, see her, and hold her hand.

Lady went and hugged the father, and Andrew, Angela, and I stood there watching. Time passed slowly, and silence presided despite the noise of the hospital. I went to the doctor and begged him to let me see Georgia, he agreed if Georgia did.

Something had happened with the arrival of the parents; the attitude of the doctors changed and became less intense. I guessed they felt responsibility toward the expat, in addition to having the embassy of Germany involved in the investigation. A while after, the doctor came to me, informing me I could see Georgia during the early hours of the afternoon. I wanted to ask him how bad she looked, but I decided to remember the Georgia I had always known before going in. Meanwhile, Lady went with the father to the coffee shop, and Andrew volunteered to go to the hotel in order to take care of things. After I came out of Georgia's room, all three of us sat there discussing our concerns and much more.

Amazing how things turn out. Does our fear of the unknown call trouble closer, or does our instinct feel the mysterious events coming? I believed it was a combination of both. More importantly, I believed our lifestyle brought reality to the surface. On the other hand, some of us foresaw the troubled patterns in others' routines and expected bad things to happen. That was the case with Georgia. More experienced people, such as Robert and Lady, had predicted the outcome, and that was my fear with the little I knew about life.

When we were faced with others' incidents, human nature reminded us of identical phases throughout our own lives. The waiting hours stretched longer than the expected time, and sitting together in the waiting room without Georgia made us lean on each other physically and emotionally and, most importantly, made our friendship and bond even deeper.

Angela started remembering her hometown and how

her father had been taken down from his position because of local conflicts. They'd had to move from one region to another, following the hierarchy order. It was complicated and dangerous. They'd left everything behind, including clothes, jewelry, personal belongings, and friends, and mainly, they'd left memories. They'd promised to go back in one month or so or after the situation settled, but the days had extended, and one month had become years. They never had gone back, and that had been eight years ago. Angela's hometown had become a fort for the rebels, and her house had become the main operational station. Her mom still carried the house key till that day, and in her mind, things were well sealed and safely protected back home, where everything was waiting for her.

After their transfer to a safe land and her dad's stationing within the new area allocated by the regime, Angela had been transferred to a new school in the midst of the academic year, which had raised more questions among her surroundings. This had made her uncomfortable. As if being the new kid on the block were not enough, she had been the descendent of a political regime that had split views in the community. She had suffered enough fear during the move, and everyone's looking at her with a question had not made her life easier and more comfy. For her parents, Angela had been a strong teenager who presented a huge support to the family. Angela was still a strong girl, but like many parents, they tended to forget how much a child could handle or what was going on inside that child's mind. That was one of the biggest dilemmas faced by children: parental expectations that were higher than their potential. Additionally, Angela wanted her parents to be at ease about her; she always felt her parents were overwhelmed with politics, and she had to stand her ground.

As Angela was describing her teenage years, Andrew interrupted her, saying, "And you think that having a dad around would make things easier?"

We both looked at him. Andrew always wondered how his life would have been if his father had been around. The lack of a father figure had left an emptiness in his journey, despite his having a strong mother by his side. Andrew never had met his dad or grandparents, and the subject of his dad always brought tears to his mom and raised a conflict with her. He did not know that his dad never had wanted to have any relationship with him, and he always blamed her for hiding that information. That was one of the things that made him explode his emotions through dance. He'd discovered he could release his frustration through dance, and his words were transmitted through the music.

His childhood had been different from that of other children. Although his mom was well known and he was pointed at as being the son of Lady, the status singled him out in the community. Lady tried to provide him with a wide social life, but while his friends were playing baseball, he was twisting on the field in his baseball uniform. He was bullied for his interests, and while the boys around him used to gather around the field to play soccer, he used to sneak to the cheerleading team and teach them steps. Soon after, he became the choreographer of the team, and he got to mingle with more girls than boys. It was tough because he could not attend all their events, but at least they shared the same interests. Thus, he had more female friends than male ones and brought few friends home. To his mom, he was a loner, but to him, he was alone.

Our interests in life draw a picture of us in society, I

thought, *and rarely can we change it. The problem is when the picture is well defined and we don't enjoy what we do.*

Andrew never hid his talent; he performed in every school event, and the audience clapped for his amazing talent. However, his mom ignored the facts and kept enrolling him in team and boy activities to get his focus elsewhere. After all, he was the son of a famous artist, an artist who struggled in building himself. In her heart, she knew where he was heading, as he had the posture of his father, but she kept hoping for a different interest. Andrew made himself. His mom's attempt to keep him away from the dance floor made him a stronger artist, because he taught himself. The struggle between the seen and the unseen developed a determined dancer in Andrew.

That was his story. Andrew displayed a clear passion for dance, and when he talked about gaps during childhood, he missed his mom accepting his talent and his dad clapping for him among the crowd. He barely mentioned the identity of his father, but he wondered if his father, if he had been around, would have accepted his choices.

Can we change our children? I wondered. *Well, it is very personal; it depends on us, the role model we play for our children, and what we are trying to change.* I believed children were born with their own genetic tendencies, and parents could barely influence them through different incidents, but they were who they were, as I was who I was. The rebel of the family could not be changed; although I lived in a small town, I dreamed of the big city. My brothers and sister conceded to my parents' lifestyle; although they were all older, they never dared to go against the flow. I was the salmon that swam upstream. Despite all attempts and my love for them, I stood behind my dream, and they couldn't take it away.

I felt hypocritical. Andrew and Angela opened up to me, but I reserved my story behind my firewall. I didn't know whether I kept silent not to be judged or to protect my daughter, Alisa, but Andrew proved to be a gentleman and just hugged me while I shed tears and could not stop. Both felt I was sensitive and, between the accident and their personal stories, fell apart, but deep down, I was thinking about my daughter, Alisa, and whether she was going through childhood phases and about my not being there for her.

Dear Alisa, daughter of mine,

You are close to three years by now and ready to start kindergarten. Please be strong. Be the daughter I would have raised myself. Don't be afraid to have an opinion or say what you want. I am sure you are well loved by the family raising you. I am confident you are well loved, because I still remember the loving girl I held when you were born. I bought you a dress a week ago. You will receive it soon. I wish I could dress you myself. I am sure you will look beautiful in it, and I hope you like purple. Till we meet again, my sweetest love.

Your mom

I always kept a copy of the written letters on me. They soothed my pain and my guilt. As I was folding the paper, Lady came with the doctor. "Are you sure you're ready to see your friend?" they asked.

I stood and walked toward the room.

CHAPTER SIX

While walking the seemingly endless hallway to her room, all I could think about was my reaction when seeing Georgia. I was praying for strength. I was praying to see the old Georgia, and my fear was in place. The doctor allowed Lady to go in with me, and at that moment, I knew I was about to see something harsh.

Georgia was lying on the bed, and her face was totally disfigured, mostly burned. She had to have reconstructive surgery once the swelling of her brain went down; she was lucky to be awake and alert. I stood strong. I stood still, not knowing whether I should or could hug her, but the minute she saw me, she started crying. She held my hand and did not want to let go; her body was scraped all over from the accident, and she was hardly able to stand, yet she held my hand tightly, as if saying, "Please stay."

Georgia and I went back years. Despite our differences in character, we had bonded. I believed expats had bonds stronger than others. We were both new in town. I had come to New York a year before she had, but I never had left the hotel till the day we met in the youth club of expats and after I had given birth to Alisa. At that time, as I saw it, my life had started.

After being with her inside the room for a while, I got used to the situation and was able to talk to the old Georgia. Lady asked me if I could stay alone with her in order to take her mom out, so she did.

We started chatting. Georgia's situation was a miracle, as the doctor said. The doctor was happy Georgia cried when she saw me; he knew I was the person she would open up to and start talking to. Indeed, before he left the room, he said, "You have a responsibility. It is called trust. We do not care about the accident anymore; all we care about now is her well-being." He then addressed her. "Georgia, you need to confide in someone, and your tears guided us to the person. Remember your friendship. It is based on trust. Part of your healing is based on getting this memory off your mind. Take your time, my dear, but fear no more investigations. Your friend is here to support you."

His words made me feel a responsibility, but I knew Georgia needed my strength more than anything else. Finally, the doctor left. The room was silent for a long time, and I couldn't come up with any conversations. Georgia was still holding my hand tightly—those were her words. Then I said, "We do not need to talk about the accident. Let me tell you about my week. I was in the hospital, then went to the hotel, showered, did not sleep, came here, met your parents, went back to the hotel, then came back here, then went to the hotel, then came here, and then the same." I started laughing, and she did too but with pain.

She relaxed and let go of my hand. She realized I had been there nonstop. She knew how deep our friendship went but never had thought I would wait on her till I could see her. I told her that Andrew and Angela were there as well, and that made her feel more loved. I guessed that was what she wanted to know.

Suddenly, she said, "I cannot see my parents anymore and do not want them in the room. I cannot hear my mom cry anymore, nor can I take her questioning. I understand her being a mom, but I know the facts will kill her. I don't know how much they know, but I hope they know only the minimum so they still think highly of me."

I told her that because her age was above eighteen and she was alert throughout the time since she came in, I doubted her privacy was invaded. She agreed, especially that her privacy was discussed with the doctor. I promised her not to ask questions, but I knew she needed to talk. Her first question was "Is the driver dead?"

I was shocked she did not mention his name, but I answered, "Dead and long gone." In my mind, I asked myself, *Why would someone want her friend long gone, unless she had a bad and terrible experience with him? She must have been traumatized instead of being able to walk away.* My thoughts were not far from reality. *One sees death as the exit only in the case of abuse. Poor Georgia, what has happened to you?*

Then she asked me if I could sleep over, as she feared being alone and did not want her mother to stay with her during the long and lonely nights. Although her stay was one long night and day, for her, having someone she could confide in was a major step toward her long healing process.

The doctor came in to see us laughing and chatting. He was happy and said, "Alexandra, feel free to stay in and sleep here. I can arrange a bed for you, and tomorrow we have a CAT scan that will define exactly the case of Georgia. If the swelling is diminishing, and it is obvious your presence is well needed and positively embraced by Georgia, we can soon start working on the physical part and start the mobility development."

We both laughed, and she said, "I just asked her to stay. I feel with her presence near me, I am fine; I even forget my pain."

So we both agreed. Then she asked about my work, and I said, "I will arrange to go to work during the lunch-to-dinner time, because life goes on, and I will come back to sleep here."

"But you'll shower here?" she said.

"Of course," I replied, "but you know me. I have to get Lady's consent."

There was a knock on the door, and Lady and Georgia's mom came in. The doctor told them about the progress he'd noticed with my being present in the room. Since Georgia's comfort zone was the priority at that stage, he recommended I spend most of my free time there, and Georgia wanted that as well.

"Lady," I said, "I will be in the hotel to take care of the lunch and dinner, but then I'll come back to sleep here."

The mother started shedding tears, and Georgia said, "Mom, it is not that I do not want you here at night, but since I am hardly able to sleep, I believe I can sit and laugh with Alexandra like old times."

The mother said, "Those were tears of happiness, dear child. It just means the old you is coming back to the surface, and I want nothing but that."

I told Georgia au revoir and went with Lady to the hotel, knowing that when I came back, the mother and father would switch with me. The agreement was perfect: the parents would get to rest; the hotel would get back into the routine, although Andrew was following on the business; and Georgia would get to heal faster.

On our way to the hotel, I told Lady, "You are the godmother of all expats. You are a wonderful person. I know you know your real value, but being there for Georgia, her parents, and me every day is a blessing; you will never understand the feeling of rushing to the unknown. I wish I had known the day I stepped out of Farmville that you were on the other side, but I guess my steps were blessed."

Upon reaching the hotel, we left the cab. Lady and I hugged. With me laying my head on her shoulder, we stepped into the hotel to see Robert sitting at our table, the table for two in the corner by the window, with a flower lying there waiting for me to smell it. He received me with a big hug, and the minute I was in his arms, I started crying and couldn't stop.

He said, "I know, my dear. I heard what happened. It is unfortunate, but—"

I interrupted him, saying, "Please don't say it was expected."

He said, "I was about to say I am glad she is okay."

I sat with him for a couple of minutes, and then I excused myself to get ready for work. Lady came and said, "Take the night off. You need it."

I said, "What I need is my kitchen." I looked at Robert and said, "I need to be in the kitchen, not because it requires my presence but simply because I need to get myself on track, so I feel continuity."

Robert understood and chose to stay and wait for me to finish. I appreciated his company. I went to my comfort zone. I was not focused at first, but shortly after, I forgot the harsh world outside and went on, creating new meals.

Lady took care of Robert; she got him a glass of wine and sat with him, chatting and explaining Georgia's situation.

As I was busy cooking, I saw a hand put a glass of wine on my table. I turned. It was Robert, and he said, "Cheers. Don't mind me. I would like to watch you involved and forgetting the world." He stood there leaning on the wall, holding the glass of wine. He was charming!

I said, "I love the way you look at me. I feel your admiration. I remember it when you're not around, and it makes me feel good. In fact, during the tough time in the hospital, I was thinking about you. I wished you were there holding my hand."

Robert smiled and said, "I miss you too, although I never used that word. I wished you were near me when I was flying. Anyway, you finish what you have to do, and I am going with you to the hospital."

My heart beat faster from joy. "Let us have dinner," I said, "and go for a walk before the hospital." Although I knew Georgia was waiting for me, I needed to see Robert. I needed his love and support before being able to love and support Georgia. It was my turn.

I prepared our dinner, sent it to the table, and went up to my room. Robert was supposed to wait for me downstairs, but soon after I got into my room to shower, I heard knocking at the door. I guessed who it was. I wrapped the towel around myself and rushed to the door, and it was him, with the dinner service and wine. "You can decide now," he said. "I can either send it back down, or I can come in, and only what you feel like will happen."

I answered through my actions: I threw myself into his arms and kissed him passionately. I missed being loved, I missed the feeling of letting go in a man's arms, and I missed the feeling after being loved. But Robert refused to take advantage of the weak time I was going through; instead, he offered a better evening: a cozy dinner *à la chandelle*. I took a shower and lay down with soft music in the background, and he massaged me softly. Then we sat there drinking, eating, and chatting. I wanted more, but he did not offer, and I did not dare ask. I felt his love and passion, but deep down, I would have gone further if he had started. I wanted to feel like a woman in love, but I guessed he was right; I was emotionally in need of a loving night, not a passionate one. We used one glass of wine, and we ate with one fork. He took care of me that night, and I felt like a princess. The love he offered was enough to get me going. I got dressed; the bottle of wine was finished; we kissed a passionate kiss; and we left the room, heading to the hospital.

The drive to the hospital took longer during the busy hours of the day. He was silent, and he had my hand on his leg, caressing it all the way. I had my eyes closed, remembering his massaging touch all over me. I did not regret that we had stopped there, because that night, when I left him, I would still want him and would look forward to our next meeting tomorrow.

We reached the hospital, and he parked the car, walked me to the room, and said, "I will be out here in the waiting room till the morning."

I did not tell him no, though selfishly, I wanted him near. I went in to see Georgia. She was thrilled to see me and have her parents go rest. Lady's driver was there, waiting to escort them back to the hotel. With tears, they left. I told them not to worry, as Georgia was in good hands. The couple of hours I'd spent with Robert gave me energy for the night, and I had a lot to discuss with Georgia. Knowing he was behind the closed door gave me a glow so obvious that it brought an abrupt question by Georgia: "Who is the guy?"

I said, "Tell me about you. You are the focus now."

She said, "Me? I missed being your friend for a while. I got lost in my own world. Tonight is your night, and I promise you that Georgia has changed, and I will prove to you with time."

I was happy to hear about the change, but I said, "I want you to be happy. I want the Georgia I first met back."

"You will hear all about the change once I know the reason behind the glow on your face," she said.

"I am in love," I said. "I don't recall the last time I felt this way. His name is Robert. He is a pilot, and he is a gentleman."

"Did you make love to him?" Another abrupt question. "I want details. I want to remember there are good guys out there. I need it to heal and stop fearing every man coming into this room."

"Oh my God, Georgia, you are safe now. No one will ever hurt you again. You are my friend." I held her hand. "I am never leaving you again to your own crazy times. We will stay together and make the future together. I assure you."

The door opened. Georgia froze and turned toward the door. It was the nurse, coming to give her the bedtime pills. Georgia said, "Promise to keep the light on."

I did. I kept talking about Robert, and within minutes, she was asleep. I stepped out and called Robert, and I snuck him into the room. I lay down on the bed, and he sat on the chair. He held my hand to sleep, and I was holding Georgia's hand to sleep. With the light on, we slept.

A couple of hours later, we woke up to howling in the room—Georgia was having a nightmare. Robert rushed out to call the nurses. I tried to wake Georgia up. It seemed what she had gone through was stronger than we'd thought. "He is back. He is back," she kept saying.

I grabbed her, saying, "No, he is not. He is far gone. You are safe."

"But how about the others?" she said.

The nurses asked me to step out. I stayed in the waiting room with Robert, and they gave Georgia a stronger medicine to calm her down.

"What did Georgia go through?" I said to Robert. "I need to know so I can help her."

Robert said, "It is far beyond your capability. Let's wait for the morning and see the swelling. Georgia needs professional therapy, but definitely, she needs you by her side."

Who is he, and who are the others? The questions needed to be answered. *Is Georgia safe or still at risk?*

The nurses called the doctor, and they placed security at the door. They allowed me to go in for five minutes but recommended that a nurse stay in with her till the morning.

I stayed in the waiting room, near Robert. I grabbed my letter book.

> Dear Alisa, daughter of mine,
>
> My sweet little soul, I hope you are safe. I cannot imagine you going through any fear with me being far away. Choose your friends wisely, never accept neglect from anyone, and never allow anyone to hurt you. I know you may not understand this letter, as the words are older than your level at this stage,

but I think one day you will, and I hope you will never need such recommendations.

Dear Alisa, pain hunts us in our dreams more than when awake. Be strong, dare to say no, and stand for yourself till I can stand for you and by you.

Love you till eternity,

Your birth mom

CHAPTER SEVEN

Who is he, and who are they? I could not stop asking myself. *It is sad how sometimes we do not know our best friend, or we lack being a best friend. I realize this is not the time to point fingers about who is right, who let go first, and who got busy. In friendship, there is no ego. Good friends remain in each other's life, and best friends get involved in each other's life.* Georgia and I both had gotten busy with our own lives.

When Georgia and I had met, we had been inseparable. We were the source of happiness to each other. I needed a friend after my leaving Farmville, my move, and my motherhood experience, and Georgia needed a friend after her move. Unfortunately, I knew nothing about Georgia's past. We limited our great friendship to the day we met and onward. We never asked about each other's past, and we both accepted each other as was. What we knew about each other we learned from the friendship circle in the expat youth club, which was a starting point for all those who were tired from their past or looking for a new beginning. That was Georgia and me, but now I regretted not knowing the real Georgia or at least the part she never revealed. For selfish reasons, I had not asked to know Georgia. I had baggage I wanted to keep closed. I wanted to keep it hidden, and I was not ready to face it. But why did Georgia never discuss her past? Did she have an untold story? Was she hiding something? Could *they* be coming from the past? Usually, people bragged about their memories; the only reason they buried a whole past was because of a phase they were trying to forget, unfortunately.

I believed Georgia's accident woke the demons up, but we would not know till the morning. Her health was the priority, but her improvement was based on her sanity. I guessed we had to wait and then start crossing off all possibilities.

I was disappointed with myself. *I should have known better. I should have embraced Georgia tighter. I am a mom now, and I should act like one, regardless of others' actions or reactions toward me. I should have known Georgia's rebellious actions were the result of an unfortunate memory; I should have asked her and stayed near. I know I had myself to care for, but as a friend, I should have raised the flag of concern.*

The morning rays rose like salvation to our long night. We had no more questions to wonder about; we had no more energy. The doctors came to inform us they had scheduled a CAT scan at nine o'clock. Additionally, they mentioned they would be happy with Georgia's nightmare if it was related to a memory. That would mean Georgia's memory was still functional—sad but helpful.

It was seven o'clock. Georgia was still asleep. Robert and I went down for coffee, and soon after, her parents joined. Robert recommended I tell her parents about the nightmare. I was hesitant in the beginning, but I did. The father was furious and started reprimanding the mother in German. The mother was in tears. Robert and I realized there was an untold story. As the doctors had said, we were happy to link the nightmare to the past, but her parents' reactions made me worry more. Had the incident in question ended in Germany, or was it related to her accident? We needed Georgia to answer the question, but whom would she trust?

Robert and I decided to wait for Georgia's CAT scan result and then leave. Close to nine o'clock, Georgia was ready to go down. She requested to see me privately. She begged me to go down with her. The doctors allowed me to be in the next room, so she would be able to hear my voice. As we were going down, Georgia said in response to my question, "They are not related!"

"Are you sure?" I asked.

"Of course, or else I would request more secure protection."

I said no more but couldn't think clearly. I decided to wait for the results and then act. But I felt responsible toward the parents, especially when a representative from the German embassy came to speak to Georgia upon the father's request, and they asked him to wait till after the results were out.

As Georgia was taken into the room for her scan, I contacted Robert and informed him of my conversation with Georgia and asked him to relay the information to the parents to ease their concerns.

I believed, despite my young age and the little experience I had, that every person had his or her own story, regardless of his or her background. I had a story as well—a long one. Some were more dramatic than others, but all were painful.

I looked at Georgia lying in there, asking her silently in my mind, *What got you here?* My thoughts were interrupted by the doctors announcing the start of the session. They asked Georgia to remain silent and not move, while they allowed me to talk to her to keep her mind off the process.

Talking to her was difficult, so I put myself in her place, although it was not easy, wondering what I would have liked to hear. I started telling her about my cooking classes, the coffee shop, and how I'd gotten involved in the kitchen. It was successful. I was able to keep Georgia's mind off the scan, but I opened a window to my own past.

As we were going back up to the room, Georgia said, "Interesting story, but no one is born walking. I want to hear all about it. It is time we get to know each other."

I laughed. "You read my thoughts. But you have to admit, we maintained a friendship despite the past." We both laughed and went to the room.

Suddenly, everyone came in but the doctors. The embassy people asked everyone to leave, local security came in, and the parents were asked in. *They* were the subject, as well as her nightmare. Although happy to know her memory was functioning properly, her parents were worried. We did not know much, except that *they* were in Germany, Georgia's life was at risk, and her exchange-student identity was a cover for her true identity. Georgia was her new name, and her last name was not the same. The only things she carried from the past were a painful memory and Germany, the country she came from. Georgia was shipped overnight by her parents under close supervision from the embassy, in cooperation with New York Police Department. She was shipped for her safety.

That was not enough for me. I wanted to hear from Georgia. I wanted to know the facts so I could help her. Had Georgia's lifestyle been the same in Germany? Had she gotten herself in trouble? There were many questions and one person with the answers. Eventually, I would be alone with her, and I would know the facts.

Georgia was too dear to me to let her live the pain alone. Together we could heal her pain, and I would help her get over it. I promised Georgia and myself I would turn things around.

Now I understood the security and investigation during the first week, but if Georgia was under such restrictions, how could she live such a trend of life? The investigation took longer than expected. Robert and I left to the hotel because we had to rest before another long day at work.

I spent the day at work wondering about life. How could someone our age stand for herself when faced with harsh situations?

Experience teaches us a lot, but to reach an experience that can make us stand our ground stronger, we need years of deceptions, incidents, and situations that we manage between tears and laughs. Are we qualified to stand for ourselves today? Does our lifestyle attract different situations? Probably yes, especially for outgoing people. Those who fear the unknown are at lower risk of facing the unpredictable. But life is not a set of stepping-stones that guide to a safe land. Every stepping-stone is a risk by itself. Are you willing to take chances, or do you prefer to hold Daddy's hand forever? Is Daddy staying forever?

I do not believe that if you go to church more often, you will fall around the right people, and as well, I believe that many of those who go to church might have abusive tendencies. Our lifestyle is measured not only by what we do but also by the people we associate with. One can get others in trouble, especially good friends. We have to stand for each other.

My thinking hurricane was interrupted by a phone call from the hospital. It was Georgia's mom, calling me to a meeting at night. I knew the meeting would tell us a lot; I felt relieved. I called Robert to join and hoped they would allow him in. No matter how relieved I was, I still lacked experience in the field of abuse, and I felt that having Robert by my side would help a lot.

Toward the end of the day, Robert came in, and I found the usual: a flower on our table for two in the corner by the window. I went to him. I was happy he felt my anxiousness. I told him about the meeting, and before I finished, he volunteered to join. I was at rest.

I finished the shift and rushed to the hospital. Lady joined us, and she was called for the meeting as well. We reached the floor, and the doctor asked us to wait outside. The parents were called, and we all went to the conference room. A lawyer was sitting there with a representative from the German embassy and another from the local authority. The parents did not mind having Robert there. They were happy to have someone older and more mature among the group.

The lawyer was about to start, when the father interrupted him nicely by saying, "This is not an official trial. We are gathering for all of you to know the history of Georgia and why she is in the States today."

The father went on. "You all know by now that Georgia has a very outgoing character. It is not recent; this has been her character since she was very young. I will respect her privacy for her to tell you her exact story, but I will brief you to discuss her security in the States. As you know by now, Georgia is not her name, nor is she using her actual last name. We are from Germany, but when I shipped Georgia overnight to the States, she was given a different name by the local authorities, and the arrangement took place through the embassy. The local authorities are working with the embassy, and they've reassured us that her accident is not related to the Germany incident. At least this is a relief to us, but why is Georgia in trouble again? This is our concern. We do not want you to betray her trust; we are happy to know that you are her friends, and no offense, but the presence of a mature gentleman among the group is very reassuring. Then again, I know my daughter, and I know that you do not fulfill her needs in terms of her character. You are her good friends but not her long night's friends. Am I correct?"

Lady took over the conversation. "I want you to know I've treated Georgia like I treat everyone, but I will not lie to you: her life trend always scared me."

Robert seconded Lady and said, "I always tried to have her end the evening and join us, but her nights started with ours ending."

"This does not mean she was going the odd way," added Lady. "She simply enjoys the nightlife, and she can afford it, while all the others within the group work and have limited nightlife."

The mother said, "You all work?"

Robert said, "I am a pilot of international flights."

"I am a chef," I said, "and taking courses as well."

Lady added, "Alexandra is a partner in Alisa's Café and the hotel restaurant; my son dances and manages the hotel; and the last one in the group, Angela, is in university and sings in our hotel to gain extra money."

Both parents were astonished with our achievements, while I was amazed at Lady for admitting for the first time that Andrew was a dancer. The mother said, "Your parents should be really proud."

Lady said, "Unfortunately, sometimes we learn the hard way; we should always be proud of our kids, especially because they will eventually learn from their mistakes."

At that moment, I looked at Lady and said, "I am lucky. That is all I will say."

Then the father said, "I want to wrap up with one question: Is there anything you want to tell us about Georgia before we let you go to her? No pressure added. Anything that you feel we need to know."

I said, "I believe what happened to Georgia was a wake-up call to all of us. We had a chance to speak only very little, but Georgia and I promised each other to be the best friends we can be."

Lady ended by saying, "Things will change now, and we will be in touch with you constantly."

The father said, "I will be going back to Germany now that Georgia is fine, and her swelling has decreased."

I started crying from joy.

"Yes, she is fine. The doctor explained her situation," the mother said. "I will remain in the hotel till all surgery processes are done."

It was time to go see Georgia. I was at ease in terms of her safety and full of happiness in terms of her reduced swelling. Although she had a long way to go to heal, at least she was safe. I went into her room and hugged her, and everyone else went home. I lay down in bed near her and asked her not to say a word, and we both slept.

In the early hours of the morning, I woke up before Georgia. I sat there looking at her, and then, as usual, I grabbed my letter book.

Dear Alisa, daughter of mine,

By now, you are in school—kindergarten. By now, you have friends who fight for you, and others fight with you. Don't let go of any of them. Friendship is a long path; it's like swimming in the mud and struggling to reach a safe land. Friendship is a cake you bake from scratch, and if any of the ingredients are missing, the cake will not rise. Do you bake cookies with your mom? I hope you do. If I were there, I would be doing so with you every Sunday.

Let me give you this recipe for a great cookie: get a big bowl, big enough for you to sit in; add three scoops of care for those you care about; add three scoops of forgiveness for those who hurt you; add three scoops of honesty for those who need to know how you feel about what they did to you; and add the three words "I love you" for those who need to be reassured that you love them no matter what. You will end up with a great cookie and the yummiest of all, called friendship. Never let go of a friend, never lose hope in a friend, and never leave a friend behind.

Love you till eternity,

Your birth mom

CHAPTER EIGHT

It was my day off at work. I sat there looking at Georgia asleep, thinking of the next time she would be out of the hospital. I decided, *If Georgia cannot go out and see the world, I should bring the world to her.* I quickly ran out, bought her favorite breakfast, and rushed back to her. I got there on time.

She said, "I thought you left."

I then informed her that I was spending the day with her. Georgia lost track of time; to her, all days were identical. Sadly, I wished we could assume the risks of our actions and try to prevent them, but I guessed we needed a strike in the face before we realized how life, our life, was.

I did learn after many strikes, but till I forgave myself, I would not heal. Life was a sequence of events that we lived and survived. Unfortunately, some of those events determined our life. I never regretted any of the events I lived or survived, and I did not feel sorry for myself. Georgia never seemed to pity herself either. That was why I never thought about asking her about her past; she always came on strong, exposing herself in different gutsy situations. Regardless, I missed seeing the resemblance between the two of us. Each of us had a story, and although different, we both were coming from a dramatic background. We might have seemed like protagonists in each other's eyes, but it took someone who lived a drama to recognize the feelings others were going through.

We sat there enjoying a delicious breakfast and discussing different issues. We started by discussing her medical improvement, when her doctor came in with the plastic surgeon. They sat with us and joined us for breakfast. It made the conversation friendlier, and they discussed the surgical procedures. We were all happy to know that her swelling had decreased like a miracle—or was it a miracle?

The doctor said, "The surgeries will take place as soon as her brain restores its original size, and if improvement remains at this level, it means surgeries will take place very soon. Georgia must gain back her physical strength beforehand; therefore, a physiotherapist will be working with her to activate her muscles slowly."

Georgia's medical condition was on the go, but how about her mental or psychological status? It was obvious Georgia was a strong girl, but how strong should one be to take on one shock after the other?

As the doctors left, Georgia said, "You will never believe how relieved I am that he's gone." Obviously, Georgia could not say two words: his name and *death*.

"You are fine now," I said. "I cannot tell you to focus on the future and forget the past, yet out of experience, I say I know what you are going through. Irrelevant of the location of the pain, there are internal scars that remain, and they are so deep that no surgery can erase them. What is important now, the priority, is your safety and your well-being."

Georgia laughed. "Yes, I wonder which should come first. You failed to mention my sanity, and I don't know if I could trust again or sleep alone again. I slept through the night last night because I knew you were here. Do you think I could ever sleep again with the lights off? Till now, the nights and days are identical to me; weekdays and weekends are the same. But eventually, when out, what is going to happen? How am I going to handle life again?"

"I beg you, Georgia, let us go through time one day at a time. You are strong, and you will stand and face the world again." I knew that words were easier spoken than lived, but I had to mention how strong she was, and deep in my heart, I knew she was.

"I keep on falling around the wrong people over and over again. I'm tired, but definitely I do not want to go back home. Alexandra, I never told you the truth and was never honest in terms of my identity and the truth about my past."

"I never asked you, Georgia. We each have a story, so please, wherever our friendship started or led us, we did not lie to each other. I prefer saying untold stories are not a lie; they are part of a past we want to keep in the past. I know we feel better if someone close knows how we feel, but it's not a crime if we keep the past private." I was talking about myself, while Georgia thought I was defending her actions. I knew it was not the right thing to do, but the priority was for Georgia to feel relieved.

She went on. "Allow me to introduce myself. My name is Gabriele. My name means 'woman of God.' Probably that is where I get my strength from. I lived most of my life in Germany. I never left it till I came to the States. I came for a reason and under the condition I would not go back. I carry a fake identity for a reason, and I'm in the hospital for a similar reason. I tried escaping my fate, which is why I am here today. I took a wrong turn and tried to face it alone. When I was in Germany, I was dating a young boy my age. Everyone said I was lucky to have him, till I ended up with sleepless nights from fear.

"We dated for like eighteen months, and we were inseparable—not because I did not want to separate. In the beginning, I wanted to be with him day and night, but later on in the relationship, when I wanted to break through, he would not let me. In the beginning, I enjoyed the care he had for me, I enjoyed the way he loved me, and I enjoyed the jealousy he felt. I explained it as extreme love, but I failed to notice his possessiveness. With time, his jealousy transferred into actions. He started following me or, rather, stalking me wherever I went, and he lost trust in me, although I never gave him any reasons or cheated on him. He started being verbally violent. In the beginning, it used to be when we were alone. Then, gradually, he did it in the presence of friends. We used to go out to public places to dance with friends and mingle with people we met there. Then, suddenly, he started wondering and questioning every act I did.

"Every time I spoke to somebody, he would question me for hours, and he even once went to a lady I was talking to, who was my friend, and compared my answer to him with hers. Slowly, he started criticizing my dress code, which could have never been arrogant or sexy, because of my father; he would never allow it. In my conversations with him, I started receiving negative, sarcastic, and demeaning answers. He started forbidding me from dancing in public. Once, I asked him to go out dancing, and he said, 'Dance here.' He put the music on loud at home and told me to dance. I refused, but he kept on yelling till I started. Then he started laughing at me and said, 'Is that what you want? You want to dance for others? Are you a pole dancer? What are you? You want to attract the men sitting there? I keep on protecting you, and you want me to fight with people.' I had stopped dancing. I was crying. He stood, grabbed my arm, and started pushing me to dance again. I was afraid and crying. I pushed him back and ran away.

"The next morning, I woke up at home with a bruised arm. It was summertime, and I was wearing long sleeves. I did not know whether I should tell my mom or not; I did not see the seriousness of the situation. My mom asked why I was pale and wearing long sleeves, and I said I wasn't feeling well. I don't know if it was the pain on my arm, the bruise, the scar in my soul, or the fear I was hiding; all I know is that I did not want to leave the house. He kept on calling. At first, I pretended to be sleeping, even to my parents, but then I started pretending to take the call while I kept the handset on my ear with the call rejected. How long could this go on? I wondered whether I was wrong and had driven him crazy and jealous, but in fact, I had not. I started doubting myself. That evening, he came to pick me up, as usual. The doorbell rang, and my mom came to the room with a bouquet of flowers and a card. The card said, 'I love you forever.' I put my clothes on and went out hesitantly, and he hugged me in front of my family, as he never had before, and we went out. He apologized all the way to the restaurant, my favorite one, where he had booked a table for two. He started telling me how sorry he was and lying about being under pressure and having lots of problems. The evening went smoothly, except I started noticing him drinking a lot.

"After dinner, I asked him to take me home, and he did, but before I went inside, he grabbed my hand so tightly that I could not pull out, and he made me promise to see him the next day and reassure him that I was not upset. With fear, I did; I just wanted to get out of the car and feel safe at home. I got home and got in the shower, not because I had to shower before I slept but because of how much I'd sweated from fear when with him.

"The next day, he made my friends call for all of us to meet. They picked me up, and by the time we got to the club, he had consumed a large amount of alcohol. He hugged me; made me sit in the corner away from everyone; and every time I intended to get up or speak to someone, he would interrupt me. I think he feared I would tell them about the incident. My fear was augmenting by the second, and my shame was as well. Everyone was begging me to dance, and every time someone did, I remembered the dancing session at his place, so I started crying. He decided to leave. I did not want to, but then I saw the rage in his eyes, and to avoid public crisis, I left with him. I begged him to drop me at home, but he locked the car, would not let me out, and started crying, saying I did not trust him anymore. Silly me—I started apologizing to him. We went to his place. I was sweating, afraid, and feeling numb; we went in with a promise from him to stay only for a short while. He threw me onto the bed and started kissing me violently, saying, 'You don't want to love me anymore. You want to leave me. You have someone else,' and he would not let me stand, get up, or leave. I pulled myself up and ran home, this time with a decision not to see him again. I ran out of the house and did not have a chance to get my purse. When I got home, my dad was awake, and he saw me shivering and asked what was wrong, but I did not speak.

"The next morning, I asked my friends to get my purse.

They all came together, and I sat with them for a short while and refused to go out, pretending I was sick. My face was red and swollen, as if I had fever. My parents started questioning our relationship and called my friends to verify their fear. They did not know anything and never had suspected anything; they thought we'd had a fight and he was leaving me, as he'd told them, and that was why I was crying that night in the club. But a mom's hunch is always in place, and my mom started questioning me nonstop. I denied everything, thinking I could handle the situation alone. Between fear and shame, I started losing weight, not eating, and going out less, and I changed my life habits. I stopped answering all calls, including those from my friends.

"One night, as I was getting dressed, I passed in front of the window and saw him standing on the street, across from the building. I was so afraid. I refused to speak to him, and again, I did not tell my parents. He was sending me flowers and gifts daily. My mom brought them to my room, and I threw them out the window, not knowing he was standing down there, which aggravated him more.

"I had to go to university. My friend called me, and she came to pick me up. I went with her because I needed to speak to somebody. During our drive, we locked the door. She wondered why, so I told her the whole story. She said he had been saying I was going through a nervous breakdown, and he was staying nearby, sending me gifts and flowers and standing under my building. I felt it was my word against his, and I felt my friend was doubting me. But when she sensed the truth in my words, she started screaming and telling me she was sorry, because he was meeting us at the university. By then, we had already parked. I saw him coming toward the car; he was enraged and drunk. I started running toward the building, and he ran after me, throwing at me all the flowers and gifts he had gotten me that I had thrown out the window. I ran with all my power to reach the security at the gate, but my legs wouldn't take me the distance; fear was holding me back. He grabbed me before the gate. The security did not notice him, as they were busy checking on my friend, who was screaming for help. She was speechless, and they could not understand the rescue call.

"Meanwhile, he grabbed me by my hair, dragged me on the floor, and took me to an empty area, where he beat me till I went unconscious. The security got there while he was about to rape me; I was unconscious. I was taken to the hospital, and he was taken to jail. I was lucky he did not have time to rape me; I was furiously beaten, though. I stayed for a week in the hospital, in a secure room, and then went home for a month until I gained my strength and was shipped to the States right after.

"He was sentenced to fifteen years in jail, but during the trial, which my dad attended, after he was sentenced, he started screaming my name, telling my father that I was his, I wanted him, I was after him, I would set him free, and he would make sure he found me as soon as he got out, because we were meant to be together.

"I never heard about him since and never want to know about him. I fear the day his sentence is completed and fear seeing him by surprise in front of me.

"Now you know the Germany story. When I came here, I was enrolled in self-defense courses, along with weekly psychology, in order to get out of my fear. That is why I disappear twice a week in the afternoon. I am still not healed, and here I am today. On my night out, I wanted to feel strong again, but instead, I am lying here more damaged than before. This guy—"

We were interrupted by nurses coming to shower Georgia and prepare her for the physiotherapist.

I told her, "You are safe now. I will be here waiting for you. I am spending the day with you. Remember, you have a new life now, and all will be okay. I promise you." But could I give such a promise?

While I was waiting for Georgia to come back, I grabbed my letter book.

> Dear Alisa, daughter of mine,
>
> More than ever, you need to remember my words. You have to trust the mother you live with. I never thought I would find myself saying those words, but again, I never thought I would give you away. Trust the parents who are raising you; they love you as if they gave birth to you.
>
> Babies are the product of love between two people and then are raised by a loving couple called parents. Unfortunately, some are not blessed to give birth to babies, but they are blessed to love a child unconditionally. You were lucky to be the product of one couple and then blessed to receive the love of another couple, who are your parents today. Love them back, trust them, and be happy.
>
> Love you forever,
>
> Your birth mom

CHAPTER NINE

The period after any phase was as traumatic as the phase itself. On a physical level, the pain caused by abusive people would heal within a specific time, depending on the seriousness of the injury, but on an emotional level, it might take years to get over the damage and be able to speak about it painlessly. Some scars would never heal, no matter how far we got on in life. The severity of both the physical and the mental injury would lessen but never disappear; it was lifelong damage. We dealt with dormant pain we tried to protect ourselves, our children, and our friends from.

But at the same time, that was the pillar of our strength and a launching point in our lives. My attitude was "Never despise the pain that taught you a lesson, for it is what made you the person you are today."

That did not mean everyone should go through an abusive period to get stronger; it simply meant you could use the pain that once held you back to make yourself immune and never feel it again. You didn't have to live your life protecting yourself; instead, you could move on in life, reassuring yourself that the pain would not hurt you again.

Words are always easier said than applied, I realized. *What matters is to find the way that makes us stronger and build on it. Each of us is different, but each is capable of standing again. Some can see the solution while drowning, while others become blinded by pain. The will to survive is a skill we all have, but we all lack practice to excel in it. There is a difference between living by the book and living by the edge, and both are based on our character. Neither is wrong, but in the eyes of the society we live in, a simple act could be considered a crime if not lived by the standard of some individuals or the community, and that is where judgment starts. Those with a rebellious character react differently to judgment, because they are the only ones who know their actions are harmless. But when those with a rebellious, outgoing character get hurt or abused, the community blame it on their character, while when someone living by the book is abused or hurt, they blame it on luck or fate.*

I believed we were all subject to abuse. Abusers had many faces, and abuse had many forms. Someone with experience might not fall for a simple compliment, but that was not certain. Those who allowed abusers to hurt them initially trusted others and believed they could change abusers along the way, and most times, the abusers had been in their lives for a while. Victims went through a cycle of guilt, self-doubt, shame, fear, stress, and being under the spell. They always believed they were in control, and then they started pulling away from their friends, as Georgia had. The abusers then felt stronger, because the victims were surrounded by fewer people. That was why friends had a huge role when confided in by victims or feeling a change in someone's attitude, lifestyle, and physical appearance, such as not seeing a friend for a while; disappearing on the same day of the week; changing food intake habits, such as loss of appetite or overeating; losing or gaining weight; changing clothing style, such as wearing long sleeves in the summertime or not wanting to change in front of a best friend; isolating and preferring to stay alone; changing social habits; and more. Sometimes those signs were just a phase, but other times, they were a cry for help. That was where good friends stood, and I had missed being that friend for Georgia.

    I was the only one who knew the real Georgia, knowing she had an odd character, living by the edge. Lady and Robert feared her character's reflection on me, so I stayed near her enough to remain in touch but far enough not to get hurt. That was not enough. I failed to keep an eye on her, and I forgot that her character would make her subject to pain by others. Unfortunately, it was a story like many others, of a young girl who survived the hard way. I thought, *Are you one of them? We all are. Each one of us struggles in a different way, and each has a story to tell. I wish sometimes we'd learn from others instead of being the story ourselves, but it's not easy, I guess. One of life's beauties is to survive an incident. That is when we feel excitement and appreciate life through survival.*

    A couple of hours later, Georgia came back. A nurse was rolling her wheelchair, and the doctor was right behind them. They all had great smiles on their faces. It was Georgia's first attempt to stand and walk. She did stand but was able to take one step only. The sign was excellent; Georgia was on her way to walking again. Georgia was lucky, as she had always been. She would get out of this dilemma physically, but when would her emotional wounds heal? Would they ever heal totally?

Soon Georgia was in her bed again, fresh, feeling the excitement of the first step. It was time to start the healing of her mental impasse. How could I help, not knowing the facts about the New York incident? *Do I want to know? I feel I owe her the truth, not because she told me her story but simply because I want her to know she is not alone; she is not the only character in the story. Georgia, dear, you have the support of an experienced woman, not just a girl, who is standing by you.* But I could not say it.

Her mom, Andrew, Angela, and Lady came to share our joy, bringing Georgia's favorite lunch. We all ate, chatted, and laughed, as we had always done, like close friends and family.

Did having family ties and friends who were like family reduce the risk of being hurt? Did opening up to friends reduce the risk of being hurt? I believed that knowing you had parents and friends out there when you needed them and had a judgment-free environment was an important factor we all needed. A judgment-free relationship was what we all looked for, since it was the first step toward trusting, confiding in people, and opening up. In life, there was no guarantee for painless relationships, since people changed, from behavior to character. *But parents and friends should grant love for free and accept you as is, love you as is, and be ready to understand you as is*, I thought.

Unspoken words are always more hurtful than those spelled out, so please understand my silence! Understand my change! Understand my running away! Understand my disappearance!

Understanding does not mean accepting but, rather,

doing something. It's a call of despair. It's a call for help. It is the call from the victim. Answer. Respond. Do something!

I looked around. They were all laughing. Georgia was leaning her head on her mom. She looked at ease; she felt safe, secure, and blessed. For the first time since leaving Farmville, I thought about my mom and dad and missed my mom's hug. Although happy for Georgia, I felt jealous. I guessed it was obvious, as Lady came and hugged me.

Lady presented me with a substitute love. I'd not thought about my parents for years, which meant I felt loved, and no doubt I was. Toward the early afternoon, while everyone was still there, I called Robert and asked him to come take me out. I needed to shower and freshen up. I told all of them I would come back in the early evening to stay overnight, and I left.

"Take me somewhere," I told Robert. "Take me somewhere I have never been to. I need to get my mind off everything."

"I understand she is your friend, and your friendship with her is very special, as she was the first person you met outside Lady's Hotel and bonded with, but you need to take things easy. Let's take you somewhere special now to get your mind off everything." Robert pulled over by the side of the road and stepped out of the car.

"Are we there yet?" I asked.

"No, just relax. If you need a breakthrough, let's make it worth it." Robert opened the rooftop of his car, gave me his glasses, wrapped my scarf around my ears, gave me a kiss on my forehead, and came back to his seat. "Are you ready now?" he said. "Enjoy the wind."

All I could think was *On the forehead? Are you serious? Can't you see the sign? I want a breakthrough with you!* Of course, I did not say that; I just enjoyed the ride with soft music.

It was a real getaway. I needed the wind. "Robert, dear, beautiful drive. I truly needed it. Thank you." I wanted to say, "You got my mind off everything through the kiss on the forehead," but I decided not to.

"We are not there yet, Ale, not yet." That was the first time he'd called me Ale. He put soft music on, put his hand on mine, and asked me to trust him and relax.

A while after, we reached a harbor. I was kind of asleep, and who wouldn't have been with such an atmosphere? When the car stopped, I opened my eyes, and for a second, I thought I was in Farmville. I opened my eyes to see yachts parked near one another next to a green meadow. It felt like a piece of heaven on earth. It had a pier of golden wood so long and wide that it would have required around an hour to reach its end. It had tables and umbrellas in the middle and covered parking to fit about a hundred cars; it looked like a private harbor. I was so taken by the sea view that I failed to wonder why Robert did not park in the parking area assigned by the boats. I stood there dreaming, and then Robert woke me up, saying, "Hey, are you there? Are you okay?"

I turned around to thank him for the ride he had given me, and I saw a mansion behind him—in fact, many of them. I froze because I suddenly knew this was where he came from. He said, "You have two choices: go to the boat directly, or visit my parents with me and then go on the boat together."

"Robert, my love," I said. It was the first time I ever had said it. It was not the mansion, the convertible, the ride, or the boat; it was simply the trip I took in my mind. "If I tell you what I want, would you grant it to me?"

"Tonight is your night, my Ale. Ask, and it shall be granted!" Robert said.

"I would like to sit here on grass, waiting for you, and watch the sunset. It is like déjà vu, and I do not want to interrupt my emotional journey."

"You can—"

I interrupted by putting my fingers on his lips. "That is my wish for now," I said.

He wanted to talk, but he couldn't slip away from my fingers. We stood there for minutes, and then I removed my fingers softly and turned around to walk toward the area I'd chosen. Robert put his jacket over my shoulders and let me walk away.

I sat there for about twenty minutes with my mind still. I sat staring at the horizon, the green field, and the ocean, and suddenly, as if someone pinched me, I asked myself the most important question: *Does Robert know?* I wished he did, but the only two aware of the details were Lady and Andrew. Lady knew a few details and had the key to my secret box, while Andrew saw everything, but we never discussed any personal issues related to me, and I doubted they would betray my privacy. *So how much of this trip is real? How come Robert never told me about his hometown?* They were questions I did not want to ask for a simple reason: to keep the past dormant. I was positive the coming evening would reveal a lot, so I decided to enjoy the moment. I started singing, and my voice reached all the hills. I felt at peace.

Close to sunset, I wished Robert were with me, and I started wondering about the time we needed to reach the hospital. I looked around. Robert was not even coming down the hill. I started to worry. Then I heard him call my name. It was coming from the sea. *It must be the echoes of the hills*, I thought. Then he pointed the yacht light at me. I was blinded by its gleam, but I followed it to where it came from. I crossed toward the yacht, feeling I was crossing to a new day. It was a change of routine that I desperately needed.

Robert received me on board, wearing a captain's cap. "Good evening, my lady. My name is Robert, and I will be your captain tonight." He grabbed my hand, kissed it softly, and then helped me in. He walked me to the upper deck, where there was a table for two with a flower on it, waiting for me to smell it, and a bottle of wine. It was similar to the table at Lady's Hotel but without the window, and this one was more romantic, out in the fresh air under the stars.

The boat sailed toward the open sea, and before sunset, the crew dropped the anchor, and Robert opened the bottle of wine. I stood there looking at how immense the sea was and wondering if I could ever reach the closest point of the horizon. Then Robert came from behind me and hugged me, holding two glasses of wine, and we stood there watching the sunset together.

The music started right after sunset, played by a band Robert had hired. They stood on the front of the main deck, and their music flew toward the skies, where the notes danced with the stars. It was a moment worth freezing. Regardless of the outcome of that night or that relationship, that moment would last forever and reenergize my soul forever.

I did not want to go back to reality, but I was worried about not getting to Georgia on time, and looking around, I felt the signs did not show that we were leaving early. An Italian chef was on board, cooking freshly in front of us; Robert said he wanted me to evaluate him for us. The "for us" was one surprise of many for the evening, but I ignored it and let it go unnoticed.

Shortly after, Robert said, "I need to ask you for one favor."

"Sure," I said.

"Can you please sing for me? I heard your voice through the valleys earlier, and that was what brought me back faster. 'How could someone be so perfect?' I told myself. I am so lucky to be with you. I am honored. Please stay in my arms and enchant me." So I did.

After I finished, Robert twisted me around, hugged me, and kissed me.

"I hate to ruin the moment," I said, "but we have to go back soon."

"No, we don't," Robert answered. "Lady arranged for someone to be with Georgia, and Georgia is aware that we are not going back. The night is ours, and we will spend it the way you choose to."

"But I don't have any clothes," I said.

Robert answered, "You won't need any."

I closed my eyes in his arms; I rested all my concerns; and to the sound of music, we danced.

> Dear Alisa,
>
> I do not have my letter book on me, but I know that tonight you will hear me through the meadows and see me through the stars. If I told you where I am now, you would say it is a fairy tale. Indeed, I feel I am the Cinderella of the evening. Do you believe in fairy tales? Well, I sure do. Read them, live them, and dream about them, because half

the dream is a reality. One day you will run toward me, and I will open my arms wide to hug you and twist you in the air, no matter how old you are, and this will be our fairy tale.

Dear Alisa, sweet daughter of mine, never stop believing. Dream it, and see it happen!

Love you forever,

Your birth mom

CHAPTER TEN

The night was still young. The chef was a keeper, but still, I had no idea of the plan. We sat there enjoying the wine and dinner, and of course, the first question was about my singing. I decided to answer only the question asked and not volunteer additional information.

"I used to entertain in a restaurant back home," I said with a smile. "A phase I am going back to. The scenery, when I was sitting alone, brought back the memories."

"When are you going to share your life with me?" he said. "I am eager to know about every phase of your life once you are ready. Now let me tell you about me. This is my hometown; I was born and raised here. I come from a family of five children, and we are all very close. My dad is the mayor; he has been for years. He's contributed a lot to this town. He built this pier, and through his connections, many rich people moved in and built houses, which strengthened the economy. He owns factories of processed food, and thousands of people are employed because of his contributions.

"Despite the richness of the town, he built the Hope Ranch. The ranch welcomes the elderly and children in need from this area and the surrounding community. It offers free shelter to those who cannot afford it, and at the same time, it is an elderly home of high caliber for those who have the resources to stay in it but no one to care for them. As for the children in need, he refuses to let any sleep in need, so he provided a public school, where they learn academics and life skills to prepare them for the outside world. He believes that children in need can shift to undesirable endings; therefore, he opened the door wide for them. My dad is a self-made man. His contributions to the society started with the Hope Ranch. As for my mom, she is a wonderful woman; she stood by my dad every step of the way and built his dream with him. Despite what five children require of her, she was the one to launch the processed-food factory, and till today, regardless of her age, she is still on top of things. As for me, I am a pilot and a sea captain. I sail for fun, while I fly for freedom.

"When I gave you the choice of meeting my parents, I am glad you deferred, because it gave me a chance to know another side of you through your charming voice, but tomorrow, before we leave, I would like them to meet you. Don't answer tonight. You will in the morning."

Dinner was over. I moved near him, and we lay down on the sun bed, covered with a beautiful quilt made by memories of old clothes, with the bottle of wine near us, under the stars. Indeed, I did not need any clothes; we were covered with romance. The music stopped; a speedboat took all the crew back to shore; and there I was, giving him more than I'd promised to.

I felt the love in his breathing, and I sensed honesty in his words. What else could I have dreamed of? I lay in his arms silently, telling myself I would not get another chance to speak up. I was fighting myself, and then the words slipped out without my thinking; I let myself go. I thought his reaction would be felt through his hug. I told him everything, from my rebellious teenage years to the singing to my background to my dream to the shameless story of giving up Alisa.

Oh, what a good listener he was, a man I truly needed. I was not wrong: his answer came from his lips kissing my tears off my cheeks, down to my neck. It only started there, and I found myself naked fully but dressed with passion. I didn't know whether I fell for him or for his reaction in not judging me, but I longed for a passionate night and, better, a night under the stars. Confessing under the stars made me feel better, not only because I needed to confide in someone but also because I felt I was confessing to God. Despite our premarital relations, I felt no wrongdoing.

Love, to me, was always a blessing. Nonetheless, in the eyes of my parents and the community, it was not accepted without marriage. I never had believed that love must be granted legally; instead, I believed that relations were based on purity, and that was what we had.

After the passionate night under the stars and the wine, I woke up early in the morning to find Robert still there, hugging me and staring at me. "Did you sleep?" I asked him.

"I never had a better night."

Breakfast and coffee were served. A lavender robe was there waiting for me and, of course, a flower for me to smell on the table for two. He gave me two kisses, one on my forehead and another passionately on my lips. "By the way," I said about the kiss on the forehead.

He smiled and said, "The forehead kiss is for the respect I will have for you forever, and any other kiss is to prove my eternal love." His words insinuated a lot, but I wanted to stick to breakfast.

We got up and enjoyed a charming breakfast, and then he asked me to go down and shower. A female helper was waiting for me and gave me the new outfit he had ordered for me: a beautiful, simple soft pink dress with a matching hat, shoes, and purse. I showered, dressed, and went up to him.

He was waiting there with a small box in his hand. My heart started beating faster. He opened the box and said, "Every time you wear them, remember me," and he dressed me with my first pearl earrings.

I kissed him and said, "Let us go meet your parents."

Till now, my story remained for him. I wondered when he was going to tackle the subject, but for now, I had a mission: to get the consent of his parents. I felt his joy, and I felt his heart beating, but my heart was beating as well. Opening up to Robert had released a lot of pressure off my back. If his reaction had been to judge or change, the morning would have been different, yet his passion increased through his actions, and that alone was enough for me.

We took a short walk to his car and drove to the home of his parents, who, surprisingly, were expecting me. *What self-confidence*, I told myself. *He knew I would accept.* Both parents received me with a great hug and a big smile, and before I knew it, I was in their kitchen, fixing desserts. We stayed till lunch, chatting and laughing. I felt loved and welcomed.

As we were about to leave, his mother said, "We are happy to meet the one and only lady Robert has ever brought home. Consider you have a family here, and we'll see you next week."

The latter was a minor detail Robert had failed to inform me about: he was inviting everyone over next Wednesday and transferring Georgia to a local hospital near the Hope Ranch, where the best plastic surgeon in New York would take care of her. I jumped into his arms, forgetting the presence of his parents, and thanked him with a big hug.

It was time to leave. We drove for fifteen minutes and then left the car, and he said, "We will take the private plane home. You have plenty of time to get back to your kitchen; stop worrying."

"I want to see Georgia first," I said.

"You will," he answered.

The night had ended, but I knew many more awaited me. He flew me over his hometown with his hand holding mine throughout. When we reached the airport at home, a car was awaiting us, and we drove to the hospital.

I kissed Georgia and told her we had big news for her in the evening, news I'd just learned from Robert that her mom and Lady already knew about and had given their consent for. Robert then drove me to the hotel and promised to come back in the early evening so we all could tell Georgia the big news.

Indeed, it had been a fairy-tale evening, but I had to get back to reality. At the hotel, Lady was waiting impatiently, not caring much for my service that day, just wanting to know about my journey. For the first time, she did not believe that privacy was due; she grabbed me as I went in with laughs and giggles. "Sorry, Robert, but she is mine now," she told him, and we went onto the roof of the hotel, a place I visited for the first time.

"Where are we?" I said.

"It is my secret shrine," replied Lady. "The only place where I can be myself, but then again, we are here to know about you, and I need to hear every detail."

Bizarrely, I enjoyed having Lady interested in my business. It was the first time ever, and it was not a choice. Lady's reaction implied she knew about the evening, so mostly, it was easy. I started talking, telling every detail since the minute we went in the car. Telling about my journey made me realize many things: I'd had a great time, I was really loved, I felt great, I deserved to be loved, and I deserved to be happy. I thought, *I do deserve to be happy. Yes, I do. I am a very nice person. My only mistake in life was being a dreamer, and who says it was a mistake? Whoever put the standards of right and wrong in life is wrong; I do not believe in right and wrong. Every action is right if we believe it is as we decide to move on with it, and as for the outcomes, if the judgment over my actions comes from a standardized community, it simply means I do not belong there.*

There will be outcomes in life that will shed our tears, break our hearts, and, most importantly, change the course of our life, but then again, are we destined from one point to the other, or are we destined to experience and choose? Well, I believe that change happens in the world through those who dare to dream and act upon the unknown, while those who fear heading toward the unseen shall remain in place and wait in the darkness for the light to go on again. If I believed in right and wrong, that would mean the nonblessed weekend that happened to me was not right. I believe that life is short and full of surprises, and every chance coming our way is worth being taken. The train will again pass by the same station tomorrow and every day, but it will not offer the same opportunity. You must look at life with your heart, not only with your eyes, because despite where it takes you, if the outcome is not with your expectations, at least you will have learned, and lessons make us stronger and more experienced.

I looked at Lady as I talked. She was sitting there holding her drink in her hand and smoking a cigarillo—a side of Lady I had never seen.

"Yes, this is me when I get a chance to be me. Martini with three olives, representing health, wealth, and happiness. Do you care for a drink?" she said.

"Only with three olives," I answered.

It was a rare moment in life to get to sit with someone heart-to-heart, knowing whatever was spoken there would remain there. That was Lady and me at that moment. Although we had shared a lot, both of us still held much back. I believed what we shared was enough to tie us together for a long period of time. *Sometimes holding back is meaningless. We think we do it for privacy or out of shame, but whatever we have done in life is who we are. Speaking about a hidden box should relieve us and make us stronger, especially because there will always be a connection between tomorrow and yesterday. Can we ever head toward tomorrow without reconciling with yesterday? Today is the fruit of a seed you planted yesterday.*

Lady and I went to the next level. I wondered if her relationship with me was related to the fact that she'd never had a daughter and never believed she would ever meet her replica in life. Daughters could be soul mates but not always full replicas, and in Lady's words, she did not think if she'd ever had a daughter that it would have been me.

I always felt that Lady treated me differently. I filled a huge gap in her solitude, as she said, yet she offered much more than to fill her solitude.

After telling my story to Lady, I informed her that I had told Robert about Alisa, and I thanked her for keeping my secret safe. She held her drink high and drank to the lady who'd walked in her shoes but dared to take a step forward, and that lady was me.

"Alexandra," she said, "everything in life starts with a baby step. As babies learn to do so, change in our life does the same. I, telling your secret, may reduce the pain of saying it yourself, but you would have never taken that first step toward forgiving yourself. You were the first person ever to know about Andrew's dad and are the only one. I praise you for taking the first step way earlier in your life than I did."

"Probably because Andrew lives with you, and you wanted to protect his identity," I said.

"No," Lady answered, "it is more difficult closing a subject when you know that answers are needed. You have a courage I never had. Always remember that."

Then Lady asked me to continue, but I had nothing left to say. She smiled and let things be.

I started talking about Georgia's move and how to tell her. Lady interrupted to say, "Don't make the mistake I made. Robert loves you and is a keeper. To Georgia now, Robert will come tonight at five, we will grab an early dinner, and then all of us will go to the hospital to tell Georgia the big news."

"I am assuming you and Robert are discussing many things," I said.

"Alexandra, my dearest," Lady replied, "no matter how much I would want to keep you forever, it is your life, your choice, and your happiness, and I will never stand in the middle."

We finished our martinis with three olives and sat

there talking about different things. Then Lady stood up, put some music on, and started dancing and twisting. I looked at her; she was dreaming, and I knew it was of Andrew's dad.

I took out my letter book. I had a lot to say and to share with my sweet Alisa.

> Will I ever have a chance to advise you in person? Oh, how much I wish you were here right now while we are having a ladies' talk, giggling and drinking. I know that life does not come on a golden tray, but I know for a fact that golden opportunities are out there waiting for us to open our arms wide and embrace them. Never fear to dream, and never fear to love what you want. What you want in life may be different from what others want and dream of. Yes, it might be, and yes, this would be the beginning of your dream.
>
> Dear Alisa, sweet daughter of mine, I wanted to keep your story a secret so it would remain mine forever. Now I've shared it with Robert, someone I love. I will never forget you; I simply shared it so I can speak about you every time I think about you.
>
> Alisa, daughter of mine and mine only, I love you till eternity.
>
> Your birth mom

CHAPTER ELEVEN

The day was about to end. I was in my room, showering and getting ready, when there was a knock on the door. I rushed to the door, thinking it was Robert, but instead, it was Lady. "I don't feel like staying alone," she said. "I got us snacks and coffee—no more drinks for now."

I sat by the dresser to fix my hair, and Lady took the brush and started brushing my hair. "You awakened long-term memories," she said. "Memories that were dormant and that I meant to bury."

"I'm sorry," I said.

"Never be," she replied. "Those memories kept me alive for years, and I do not want you to go through the same; I want you to have a life and not worry about tomorrow. I want you to be happy and follow your heart. When Andrew's dad left me, I shut my heart down and buried all my feelings. I cried myself to sleep for days. The difference between us is that I was financially secure. Many approached me for friendship and for relationships, but back then, it was seen as very unethical to be a single mom. I limited all acquaintances to business encounters and never let myself go beyond work. I am sure that had I allowed myself to go beyond, I would not have stayed single till today. One day I sneaked an evening out. I was very lonely. It was Christmas, the hotel was booked with families, and loneliness broke my heart. There was this guy—"

Suddenly, we were interrupted; someone was at the door. I opened it, and it was Robert. "You were not down. I miss you," he said.

Lady said, "Come in. We never went down today."

"I ordered a bottle of champagne," he said. "Before we go to the hospital, I will call it up."

"Meet me on the roof," said Lady, and she left.

Robert sat by the window, watching the sunset, while I finished. Then we both went up. "Where are you taking me?" he asked.

"To a piece of heaven," I answered.

Lady was already up with the champagne and, of course, the flower Robert had gotten me. We sat there.

"Indeed, a piece of heaven, the rooftop," said Robert. "Allow me," he told the waiter. "It is my honor to open the champagne for the beautiful ladies," and he did. "How come this place is a secret?" Robert asked.

"I needed a place for my thoughts," Lady said. "A place where I could live my life."

"No more solitude," said Robert as he raised his glass to us, "and I will not say more for now."

Lady had dinner ordered, and she stayed with us for a while and then said, "I am going down to check on the restaurant, and when you finish, we'll go to the hospital."

The setting felt too romantic to let go of, but we had to go see Georgia. We took the elevator down, and Robert grabbed me close to him and kissed me as he never had before. "Should we go up again?" he said with a smile, "I miss you so much. I want to hug you and kiss on you from head to toe, but I do not dare, fearing you might think that is what I want only. I need more than a ride up to quench my feelings."

"Let us go see Georgia, and then we will have the night for us," I said.

"I will be traveling early in the morning," Robert said. "I will be back in two days."

It was news I did not want to hear, but too much was going on: Lady's story, Georgia's announcement, and his parents' dinner. It was too much to handle, with me sinking in emotions, wanting him every minute. We reached the ground floor, met Lady, and went to the hospital.

"Ale," said Robert, "you should be the one to announce the news to Georgia. The doctors are there by now, waiting for us. I believe no matter what she hears, knowing you will be near her during the process will ease her concerns."

"Ale," said Lady, "if not exclusive, that will be your name from now on, and yes, I agree with Robert."

Within thirty minutes, we reached the hospital. Andrew and Angela were there with Georgia's mom and the doctors. I hugged Georgia, and when she saw new doctors, she started crying. "Bad news?" she asked.

"No, dear," I replied. "The exact opposite. I will have the doctors explain the procedures; then I will do the rest."

The doctors introduced themselves and the most recent plastic surgery mechanisms, and then I took over. "The operations will not take place here; you will be transferred upstate, near Robert's home. I will be with you till you ask me to leave. I promise. The results are worth the move; it is a beautiful place, and you need the change."

"How do you know?" she asked, and we all laughed.

Robert hugged me and said, "You will have plenty of time to hear about it over there, only if you agree we can transfer you. I promise you are in the best hands one can have."

Georgia agreed and signed the transfer papers.

Robert added, "A helicopter will transport you early in the morning. Your mom and Ale will join you."

"I will not go without Ale," she said. "Ale—I like that."

"I will see you in the morning, sweetie," I said, and we all left.

We went back to where we'd left off at the piece of heaven on the hotel rooftop. Robert and I spent the evening there. Time I spent in his arms flew by faster than the speed of light. *Should I hold myself back, or should I let myself be guided one more time by love and passion?* The usual me would have followed her heart, let passion penetrate deep in her soul, and followed her feeling. I decided to take the initiative and embark on a love trip. I looked at Robert lying on the sofa bed relaxed, holding his glass of wine, with eyes closed. I felt the urge to surprise him and make him happy. I remembered his words "I want to kiss you head to toe," so that was where it started. The evening went on, and lust was in the atmosphere. *I guess when you love truly, making your partner happy becomes a natural action.*

We stayed there till the early hours of the morning. Robert had to leave, and I had to sleep. "I miss you already," he said, and with those words, we ended a passionate weekend and swapped to reality.

The reality was, we all had to stand by Georgia to start her off on her healing journey. Early in the morning, I went down to my kitchen, fixed my coffee, and prepared many dishes that would help the chef during my absence. Then I joined Lady for coffee. Knowing that Georgia was on her way to better service for her case made us both feel better. We also discussed the hotel and my being away during the last period of time. Lady felt Georgia should be my priority, but I reassured her that my priority was and would remain our business. Georgia was in good hands, and her mom was near. I said, "But we have a business to run. I will fly weekly to spend the day near her and will talk to her about it after the surgery. Anyway, mid next week, we have the luncheon at Robert's parents', and we still have a lot to talk about."

I knew Lady's fears were beyond the next couple of weeks. I knew she was worried about losing me, but I had no choice but to let time be and judge my actions toward love and life.

My ride was there to take me to join Georgia. I hugged Lady and said, "A dream is never over till we say it was fully and successfully accomplished."

She looked at me with a smile, but we both knew that talk was premature, and we were not ready to toast for the decision yet.

I took the ride to the hospital, where they were in the process of moving Georgia to the rooftop for the helicopter ride. Her mom was there with a group of doctors and nurses. Georgia was happy and worried at the same time. Her mother looked at me and said, "It is you she needs now. I have my own ride down waiting for me. We have a saying in Germany that says, 'When your child's friends are here, know better, and stay out of the way,' so she is all yours, and I am happy she has you."

All on board, we left. "We should have taken this trip not to the hospital and way before everything happened.

We did miss a lot. Remind me next time not to miss a moment," I said.

Georgia laughed and replied, "Moments. I wonder when they will come back again." Georgia's health, on a physical level, was normal. Her brain was back to normal size, and she was able to walk normally. The visible harm was in her facial appearance, and the severe damage was on an emotional level. Any joke we said or anything we mentioned would take her to regret. She was in a critical phase. She thought poorly of herself and was concerned about the success and outcome of the plastic surgery. Georgia was a beautiful lady, in addition to loving attention and ensuring that she got it. She never failed to get what she wanted, and for that, I always had admired her.

We each get satisfaction in different ways, I thought. *Sometimes it does not suit the community, our close friends, or our parents, but to us, it means a lot. As long as it does not stand in the way of our success or our goal, in that phase of young adults meeting our potential, it is simply important to nurture our ego.*

In life, we go through phases, and those phases determine our future. Some might teach us trust, love, care, selfishness, strength, lies, motherhood, reality, peace, and passion, and others might teach us about abuse, drugs, hatred, the value of money, dreams, the cost of happiness, and family.

Mainly, everything we learn in life we learn at a vulnerable age, during adolescence and early adulthood, when we mostly need to learn about values, and we get slapped.

Georgia, was a nightaholic, while I was a workaholic and a dreamaholic. She never had enough at night; she loved the nightlife, and all her problems started at night, while mine developed during my dreams and through my love for work.

"Georgia, my bestie," I said, "you are a nightaholic, and you need to use that as a strength. You need to build on that when you are back on your feet. You need to think about the future now, because once you are out, you will have no time to think. I will not let you; you have to find your strength among the downfalls and build your future. Let us discuss the future, no more past."

"Are you sure he is gone?" she said again. "Are you sure he is no longer coming back? One of the reasons for me to accept the move uptown is to be farther from the area that hurt me. I want to feel safe and secure. I agree with you. My nightmares started during the long nights, but they always hunted me during the daylight, and that is one of the reasons why I rejected sleeping during the nights. I felt security while awake in the darkness; therefore, I rejected the nights. When I met him, I met him at night. I never knew he was a drug addict. I never knew he had two personalities. The first time I woke up near him, I ignored that I was drugged; I thought I did it willingly. Soon after, I realized. He inhaled more drugs than air. He was fun to be around, and then one day, when I pretended to drink, I realized that was how he used to drug me. I realized how bad he was. I understood then the bruises all over my body and how I received them. I was scared because I was alert and not under the influence.

"I decided to heal him. I thought he was a gentleman. He kept telling me I got the bruises while dancing, but the reality is, I got them in bed because of his violence when under the influence. Sadly, I knew the truth when I suspected he was drugging my drinks; no wonder I became addicted to alcohol. It was worse; it was drugged alcohol.

I lost the baby he wanted me to abort, but who would want an addict and an abuser as a father? When I tried to help him, he refused to admit he needed help; he insisted he was in control and could control it and stop it anytime. So I hid his box of drugs once, and when he couldn't find it, not knowing I had hidden it, he became violent and started breaking things around the house. Then I put my hand on his shoulder, not knowing you cannot approach a violent man. He pushed me, not caring where I fell, and kept on looking.

"Being so afraid, I started looking with him and found the box for him. 'You misplaced it,' I told him.

"He laughed and said, 'You will get a treat tonight.' I thought the treat was a calm evening out; instead, he wanted to inject me—something I had never seen or witnessed before. I refused; I was scared. I took the motorcycle keys while he was injecting himself, which gave me time to run out of the house. It turned out that after the rage, he regained a strength I had never seen or known about. He ran after me and got on the motorcycle behind me. 'You want to play?' he said. 'Let's play.' He took the motorcycle helmet off my head and bit me on my ear so hard it started bleeding. From fear, I accelerated the speed. He said, 'Faster. Go faster. Feel the blood heading up to your brain.'

"The only thing I was feeling was fear. I had blood all over my shirt, and my hands were shivering. He put his hands on mine and put the motorcycle on high speed. I was screaming from fear, begging him to stop, promising him to stay and not run away again. 'You wanted to feel the rush while speeding,' he said. 'Feel it.' Then we faced a truck coming; we were on a curve on the mountain. I closed my eyes; I knew it was the end. I put my life in

God's hands and started praying. The next thing I knew, I woke up in the hospital, not knowing whether I was alive or dead and mainly wishing to be dead if he was still alive.

"When I woke up, the doctor told me, 'I have bad news: you lost the baby,' while all I wanted to know was if he was gone. Then I heard the news. I did not know whether I should be happy or cry. Bottom line, I was relieved. I wanted to see his end."

"Oh my God, my bestie, I am sorry I was not there for you," I said.

"You couldn't have been. Don't blame yourself," Georgia said. "I have only myself to blame. I should have known better. I should have known that addicts need professional help. I should have known to drop out when I wondered about my bruises. I should have known that alcohol addiction has different symptoms, because I wasn't drinking to be out. From now on, I will remember one thing: when out at night, drink to have a memory; don't make the relationship a memory. I want to forget. I want to erase it all from my mind, and I want to be happy and safe."

The captain announced the arrival to the hospital uptown. All I wanted was to see Robert. I couldn't spend the night alone. The fear from the night and strangers hit me.

We got there, and they took Georgia in to make her comfortable in her room. Her mom went with her, and I sat in the waiting room, waiting for a familiar face. I grabbed my letter book to talk to the only close person in my life whom I could feel during her absence. I looked at the mirror in the waiting room and then wrote.

Dear Alisa, sweet daughter of mine,

I need you to hug me right now. I need to feel secure, and I need you. I wish you were sitting with me. I wish life had treated me differently. The only fear I have right now is for your adoptive mother not to understand your fear. Let them know what you think. Let them know you fear the nights if you do. The only fear you should have is not to be understood, and that is why you should tell them about your thoughts. Write them down, draw them, and get things out of your mind.

Be happy. You deserve to be. You are a wanted baby. You are the fruit of love between two people, and that alone is the gift of life.

Love you forever and unconditionally,

Your birth mom

CHAPTER

TWELVE

The next days were tough. I felt lonely and scared. Robert's parents were there, and Georgia's mom was there, yet I felt lonely, and I needed Robert. I lost track of time, and I couldn't remember when Robert was due back. The plastic surgeries started, and too many changes were happening all at once. I was scared. Although all symptoms were positive, I could think only about the fear Georgia underwent and how much the doctors knew about the whole ordeal. I decided to speak to the psychologist of the hospital. I did not know any better, especially as I did not know how much Georgia's mom knew. Georgia had a long way to go to heal on a physical level, but how about on the emotional one? Although she had been seeing a shrink back in New York, I knew she had stopped during the last relationship, when she'd needed him the most. How much could one take, how much fear could one endure, how many relationships could one survive, and how many failures could one live and still keep faith in self and others?

Why was there so much pain and cruelty in the world? Why was goodness sometimes lost and in vain, and why were we always falling around the wrong people? I believed schoolchildren should be taught self-defense, and I believed all kids should be tested for psychological concerns. Were those abusing others retaliating against their past? Were they aware of their actions? Was there a difference in cruelty between emotional and physical abuse?

I believed in zero tolerance for abusive people on any level, physical or emotional, and felt they needed to be treated following a court order and locked up. I was not harsh; I tried to be in the shoes of those who were abused and tried to feel their pain, feel their fear, and imagine their faith in self and others. How could we ask someone who was abused to move on in life normally? How could we ask them to be strong, face other situations without hesitance, build new relationships, fall in love again, and feel safe and secure? How could we tell a victim not to base the judgment of the future on past incidents or link the newcomer to the old one?

I did not blame Georgia for her reactions nowadays. Although her love for the nightlife, in the eyes of some members of the community, led to her trouble, that did not give anyone the right to hurt her. Some of us enjoyed loud music, dancing, drinking, and the night lights, while others preferred quiet evenings or staying home. Neither was wrong; none of those choices were hurtful toward self or others or calls for trouble. *We should feel safe and be safe*, I thought. *Sick people should be locked up. Our choice of social life is strictly our business and reflects only on us. Both successes and setbacks relate only to the person who undergoes the clashes.*

I had great respect for Georgia's parents for maintaining

their trust in her and showing it. They knew Georgia was far from being locked up or retained; she had been born with a free soul, a soul that soared like an eagle, and no one could break a soul. With all the pain she was going through, I envied her for her parents' understanding. I was not jealous but was happy for her, and I wished my parents were understanding toward my dream. I was a parent, and once a parent, one could not stop being a parent. Although I'd chosen to give away Alisa to a family who appreciated her and I had full faith in Lady's choice of parents, I felt I had duties toward her, and I believed that fate would cross our paths one day, and I would offer her my support. Additionally, one day I might be blessed with a child I would raise, and dreaming was the first step I would teach him or her.

Those who have no fear will stumble way more than those who study their steps, and they will fall many more times than those who secure their decisions, but they also will shine more than others. Lessons learned through personal experiences are the life lessons taught and mastered through personal experience.

Those who have no fear will stand faster than those who worry about the unknown, for they have inner strength that pulls them back up to stand and even to stand alone. This is Georgia, the fearless woman young in age but aged in strength. What determines our age? What we have accomplished on our own. Our accomplishments are the sole realization of our dreams and what we have done without being guided or given a handbook delivered by others, mainly our parents. Our dreams carry our initials; they take our soul high; and before we hear the words "I am proud of you," words we all look up to, we love the "I take pride in doing so and so."

Despite the analysis I reached while thinking about Georgia, I was still possessed by fear and needed to see the shrink. I called for a session, which was offered directly to those standing by Georgia. The doctor was a lady. I was glad because I felt it took a woman to understand another. Many might have disagreed, but it was my comfort zone. I went into her office, where the color of lavender was soothing. There was nothing there to distract my thoughts, other than a saying: "You are now at home." It was a huge office that had only two lounge chairs, not even a desk. Her work station was in another office. I lay down there. It felt like paradise, and my first question was "How long may I stay?" I felt comfortable, and my mood changed. I said, "Do you know what, if I had passed and were sitting in heaven, would be my thought? I would first wonder if this is truly heaven, because I lost touch with the only thing I wanted to discuss: fear."

"Fear is part of reality," she said. "You feel detached here, and therefore, you feel safe. What are you fearing?"

I replied, "The past and not the future. How can I fear a past that is no longer part of my tomorrow? How come incidents that happened to me, incidents that I overcame and faced already and that were memories I never thought about for a long time, came to surface? Those memories never hurt me in the past, but today I am fearing. I am afraid they will come back to haunt me and hurt me."

"Dearest Alexandra, you must have had time to think about the past lately—time you never had before," she said. "Our memories go into deep sleep, and they are revived through current incidents that make us wonder about our life. Did you live a change of life pattern lately?"

"More than I deserve, and I know I deserve a lot. With Georgia's accident, I am thinking about the pain in the world and my loved ones. With a recent love, I worry about losing it. And with Georgia's parents' reactions and support, I wonder if my parents had offered me this support, would I be here now?"

"How come you are not discussing your work?" she asked.

"My work is secure," I said. "I worked hard, and still am and will, and mainly, I trust Lady."

"Do you not trust the others?" she said.

My thoughts were directed to Robert. "I trust the love I feel, and to me, it is real, but people change, and what if?" I answered.

"Do you believe anything is one hundred percent secure in life?" she asked.

"If I failed the only person I should never have, the answer is no," I said. "How could this person live with faith and trust others while knowing the beginning was an act of abandonment?"

"What do you mean? Would you like to talk about it?" she asked.

"Not yet, not really, and never," I answered.

"Before we wrap up, would you like to come back? Because if you do, I have an activity for you," she said.

"Let me take the activity, if you don't mind, and then I will decide," I answered.

"No problem. Here is what I want you to do," she said. "I want you daily to mark on small pieces of papers five things you may have questions about and then five things that made you happy that day or any time before. Please do not write them on the same paper, and please do not read them at any time. Put them together on a daily basis in a bag, label the bag by date, and seal the bag. When ready, no matter when, bring them to me."

"I will write them, and who knows? I might come back," I said.

I left her office with peace, but the minute I closed the door, the anxiety came back. I guessed I was not comfortable when surrounded by emptiness. I noticed that despite the incidents taking place around me and my being worried about Georgia, my only comfort zone was when I was involved at work.

Luckily, I saw Robert standing in front of me. I rushed into his arms and burst into tears. "Ale, my love, are you okay?" he said. "You had me worried. I have been searching for you for the past hour. What is wrong, my Ale? Tell me. Let's go elsewhere."

I couldn't speak; I was fully down and emotional. He took me to the car, and he kissed me on the forehead and then on the side of my lips.

"Don't leave me tonight. Please don't," I said with tears dripping nonstop.

"I won't, my love. Sorry I wasn't here for you, my Ale. I should have known better and canceled my trip," he said. When I sat in the car, my flower was there in front of me. "I will never change," he said. "You are my Ale."

If I had not met him by the door, I would have said the shrink had told him about my fear, but no, his words reassured me that he was real and a genuine person, at least for now.

He drove me to where I had sat and sung. It was early evening. He got a cover from the trunk and laid it on the grass, and we sat there. He said, "Let us watch the sunset from here." He put his jacket over my shoulders.

Oh my God, I told myself, *déjà vu*. But then I said to myself, *I will not allow a bad apple to make me hate apples*. I shifted my mind from Farmville memories with Alex back to the current time, back to Robert.

He hugged me and said, "I am here now and not leaving you again till you tell me it is okay to do so. Ale, my love, be strong with everyone else, but when with me, I want you to be yourself. It is okay to be weak. Weakness is a sign of sensitivity, and people only cry when they have been strong for too long and have no one to lean on. Lady stood by you in the past, and she will never let go of you; she loves you as a daughter. You stood by her as well—as a daughter, as a friend, and as a person she longed to have in her life. Never change that, but when it comes to me, I want to be the person who supports you, the shoulder you lean on, the man in your life."

I put my fingers on his lips and kissed his lips passionately, still with tears dripping. I rested my head on his shoulder, still not able to speak, and then slowly, I said, "Thank you for being you."

We sat there for a couple of moments silently, but our hearts said much more. Soon after, I calmed down. I looked him in the eye, and he said, "Tell me what is wrong."

"Honestly," I said, "I needed you. With a hospital full of doctors and loved ones around, all I could think of was that you were not there. Too many things happening. Georgia opened up to me and told all that had happened with her. It brought my memories up to the surface, and I discovered that work is my comfort, but I haven't been working. Nothing could keep my mind busy, and you weren't here."

He smiled and said, "I am here now. Georgia won't want for anything in the near future. She has all the accommodations she requires, including her mom and my mom, and all is fine. It is you I am worried about, and I promise not to leave you." He then contacted his office and told them he was off till further notice. "Where would you like to sleep, my Ale?" he said. "Home, the hotel, or the boat?"

I chose the boat. I needed him selfishly for me only that night. So there we went. He kept the boat parked, and we stayed till passion drained out of us. Then we slept.

The next morning, when I woke up, he was not near me in bed. I put my robe on and went up on the deck, where he had breakfast ready. As we were eating and having coffee, the phone rang. "For you," he said.

It was his mother, asking me about the buffet and what ingredients I needed. "You are cooking, right? My kitchen is yours."

I laughed and said, "Sure."

After breakfast, I asked Robert to take me to the market. On our way, he said, "I did not ask my mother to call you; she did it from her heart, and no one is allowed in her kitchen. Ale, my love, time will prove to you who I am, and I will gain your trust. I know I will."

The market trip was wonderful. His mother met us there. We were chatting and laughing, and more longing for my mother ached in my heart.

While we were shopping, his mom said, "No worries. I will leave the kitchen in your custody. I will not steal your recipes, not even when you launch your personal department in the factory."

I froze and looked at Robert, and he said, "Sorry. My mom blew the surprise, but yes, we are giving you your own department, with your consent and following your terms. It is your birthday gift. Let's us enjoy the lunch today, and we'll discuss things later."

I went on shopping and got my ingredients, and then his mother hugged me and left to meet us at home. While

Robert was taking care of the bill and having the groceries transported to the car, I sat there waiting for him, and I grabbed my letter book.

Dear Alisa, daughter of mine,

By now, you are about eight. Probably you are wondering about the reason why I gave you away. Well, I do regret it every minute of my life, but I cannot take away from you the right to be loved in a home by a mother and a father. I wonder if you have sisters and brothers. They are precious, you know, regardless of all the fights you go through together. My dearest daughter, and the only one I gave birth to, parents want the best for their children, and if you cannot be with your child and give them what they deserve, out of love, you have to let someone else do it. When I had you, I was young and barely able to take care of myself. That alone was enough to find you a home. Lady, my friend and guardian angel, chose your home for you. I trust her judgment and am confident you are in good hands. Never doubt my love for you.

Love you till eternity,

Your birth mom

CHAPTER THIRTEEN

My heart froze at a specific point. I didn't know whether it was beating so fast that I could not feel it or had stopped and now I was in heaven. *Is happiness real? Does happiness have a cost that I have to pay at a specific time, or have I done something good in my previous life and am being rewarded?* In my previous life, I might have, but in this one, I expected punishment. No one let go of her own flesh and blood and expected to be rewarded. But I had done it for my daughter's own good, for her to be blessed with a better life, live in a healthy and happy atmosphere, and be loved. I'd given her away to a family who could offer her a chance to live her childhood, her dream; I'd refused to take away her soul from her, and most likely, the family she was with had wanted children. *I should stop myself from living the guilt.* Lady reassured me that Alisa was in good hands, and she offered to give me details, but I refused so I was not tempted to see her and disturb her serenity. *I should move on, I should enjoy the moment, and I should let a higher power be the judge over my actions when the time is due.*

Robert was driving the car, holding my hand, but I was distant; I did not feel his hand.

"Ale? Hey, my love, are you with me?" said Robert.

I looked at him. "Of course, my man," I said. "Always."

"What were you thinking about? What is bothering you? I am sorry about the way you heard about the surprise. I wanted to discuss the plan with you, but my mom thought you knew. It was her way of welcoming you; she just wanted you to feel at home and comfortable."

"It is Alisa I am thinking about, my love, and probably feeling so close to your mom reminded me that mine is not around. Are you sure you want to be with a tormented soul?" I said with a smile.

"I want the full package, and most importantly, I do not want you to let go of your past; it will always be part of you, with you, and with me. Once you are ready, we will discuss it," Robert said. "I respect your privacy, and I am keeping your secret deep down in my heart. Ale, my love, you are not alone; you are well loved and surrounded by people who appreciate you and your dream. I am here to stay, and our future is in your hands and upon your service. Don't let yourself sink into a past where many people unintentionally got you where you are. I am positive your parents did not want you away and out of their life, but you have to understand the background you are coming from. You did the best you could at a time when it was the best you knew how. Stop blaming yourself for any outcome. You owe it to yourself to be happy and enjoy whatever comes your way that makes you happy. Cheer up, my love. I beg you to speak to me and not shut me out of your thoughts. Two minds are better than one, especially if they have joined their hearts. I love you, my Ale. I love you till eternity."

I looked at him. "That is exactly how I feel, and that is the same thing I tell Alisa every night. Take me home, dear. Let me sink in the kitchen, and let us have a great day," I said with joy in my heart and a kiss on the side of his lips.

We reached his home, and everyone was out and busy, setting the tables in the garden, tables for way more than eight people. "Not to worry," Robert said. "I added more ingredients and doubled the quantity. My parents invited all their friends in honor of a great chef from New York."

His parents rushed to welcome me again, and along came Lady, Georgia's mom, Andrew, and Angela. To the side, staff were setting up a small stage. I looked at it, and Robert said, "It is for Angela; she wanted to entertain us." I smiled, hugged him, and then went to the kitchen.

That place was another world. Robert's mom had a full team at my service. The chef I'd met on the boat was there to assist me, and there was a group to take care of the service.

"How many are we expecting, and at what time?" I said.

Robert's mom answered, "About sixty, and they will start arriving around two."

I called Andrew in and asked him to take care of the welcome drinks, guests' tables, and buffet area; meanwhile, Angela supervised the entertainment. It was ten o'clock in the morning. I was busy preparing the start-ups to facilitate the work, when I felt someone staring at me. I turned, and it was Robert. My heart said, *I adore the way I feel when you look at me, and I want you now*, but my mind said, *Let me work*.

His eyes answered, *I love you. How I would love to love you now on the kitchen floor.* Then he said, "Keep on working. I am admiring the master at work, waiting to see your hors d'oeuvres come together, but whenever you can let go for half an hour, let me know."

Shortly after, I removed my robe and apron and went with Robert. He walked me to the upper floor and crossed a glass passage over the garden to reach a big wooden door. He opened it, and I stepped into a small garden and then through another door to a cute little apartment. We walked to the last door, and there was the bedroom, with a bed, mirrors, and curtains flying, and a dress lay on the couch. It was a long black dress, and knowing Robert, full accessories were ready.

"I love it," I said.

"This is our suite, if you would ever consider sleeping here. Full privacy, a separate entrance, and connected whenever we want to. You need to be dressed by two. Everything is ready for you."

I walked slowly toward Robert, moving us back toward the bed. He sat, and I sat on his lap and started kissing him and said, "That is what I was thinking about when I first saw you."

He smiled and said, "I love the way you initiate things." Then I felt his hands rubbing my back, my skin, all the way down to my toes. His lips were all over my neck and ears. I was not thinking anymore. My body, soul, and feelings were synchronizing and sinking, vanishing in a world of passion. Those who did not dare to love would never find love.

The phone rang. I was called to be in the kitchen. I stood up and kissed his forehead.

"On the forehead?" he said. I gave him another on the side of his lips, and he smiled.

"I cherish you, my man."

"Ale," he said, "you are my Ale." I left him there to nap.

Back in the perfect kitchen, everything was white and silver; it was a piece of heaven on earth. My thoughts about the chef had been in place: he was a keeper, even though I was not aware of what was coming next in the day.

Close to noon, everything was falling into place. I told the chef I was going to get myself ready. I went up to the room to find Robert in bed where I'd left him, lying there enjoying the music, except there was no music; those were the pulsations of his heart.

He looked at me and said, "I think I might like you a little."

"Only a little? You think you might like me?" I said. "Well, I have to love you harder then to make sure I gain your love. But we need to get ready."

Of course, we had to shower before getting ready, and looking at the bathtub gave us more temptations, especially as Robert was not done feeling and loving me, but we looked at each other and said, "We have to get ready."

Down in real life, the chef had everything under control, and Andrew was handling the welcome service part. We heard the music, but this time, it was real music.

We were both ready to face the music. "Good luck," he said.

I did not know what he meant. "But I have it already," I answered.

Robert's family were well connected, not only on a local level but all the way to New York, Los Angeles, and Europe.

We stepped out into the garden, which was crowded,

and started greeting people. Among the crowd were food critics, restaurant owners, and event organizers, and only few were family. I looked at Robert, and he said, "This time, I am speaking before my mom, although it was her idea: the launching of a high-caliber catering service. My Ale," he said while holding both my hands and facing me, "I am not trying to pull you out of New York or away from Lady or Alisa's Café; they are special to you, and anything special to you will become special to me. But I want you to see the dream you barely told me about growing. I want you to trust that I am not changing you but want you to grow, and I want you to trust that I will not change. On this, I will let time be the judge." He ended the conversation with a kiss on the forehead and another on the side of my lips.

After we greeted everyone, lunch was served. I was scared, as if I were passing a test at school. Robert's dad interrupted the singing to make a toast and break the ice, saying, "I would like to take a moment of your time to remind you that this gathering is to celebrate the beautiful people in our life, including our lovely Ale. Remember that the most important thing in life is to do what you love best with those you love best. To family and friends. Cheers."

Robert looked at me and said, "I do."

I looked at him questioningly.

He said, "I do what I love with the one I love."

The entertaining went on. People were eating and taking notes, and back in the corner, Lady, Georgia's mom, and Robert's mom all were looking at me but each with different thoughts, and some were unexpected. Robert and I walked toward them.

"You are the star of the evening, my dear, and the star shining upon my son, and I am glad he is in good hands,"

Robert's mom said. "Let me tell you a story about my life but in brief because you don't have time tonight. I started my life against the flow. I followed my heart. I tripped many times, but my heart was as strong as my will. I stood again. Although you might hear that I did it alone, I had full support in the background. I take pride in having such support; it is the kind that will not take away your credit. Most importantly, in life, trust your heart. At least you will enjoy what you are doing."

Wow, I said to myself. *Such a statement from someone who knows I am dating her son. She said it to me, a person with a history of pursuing her dreams. First and foremost, she must be a genuine person. Two, she really likes and appreciates what I am to her son before what I am doing to the business.*

Then Georgia's mom said, "I am proud of you. For someone your age, putting such a feast together, you have a talent and not only in the kitchen. You were able, within the same-day preparation, to ace an event. You must have great potential. This does not require cooking skills only but also organizational skills. I do not want to discuss Georgia, although she is my daughter, my love, and my pride, no matter what she gets herself into. Simply, I want to say I am happy she has a friend like you. Never underestimate the ability of a woman with a good heart; she can rock the world."

Wow, again, am I awake? But I was proud of myself for such success.

Last, it was Lady's turn. "Since the first day I met you, I never told you that I stood there watching you throughout the evening. It was like ten years back. You were young but standing there like a rock in the wind. While the boat was rocking and the wind was blowing, you were there with full will, dreaming, while you should have been worried about the unknown. I said to myself before talking to you, *This is a girl determined to reach her dream.* You were amazing, hiding your fear and showing the world no scars. It takes one to know one, and I knew the kind of person you were at that moment. The decisions you made next in your life would make anyone around you admire your strength."

Robert squeezed my shoulder in approval.

Lady continued. "Never fear what your heart tells you, because despite the tears, fear, and uncertainty of the future, I believe the universe is by your side, not only those who love you. I have the right more than anyone else to say you are one of a kind, because truly, you are. This is only the beginning of a great future. Keep believing in yourself, because I believe in you."

Then Robert said, "I think I am a very lucky man. Three testimonials that must be documented. My Ale deserves all that and more. Let's go around."

As we were walking, an older guy with a white mustache came to us. "Alexandra it is, right?" He was holding a pen and a small booklet. "How do you do it?" he asked.

I smiled. "What? The food?" I said.

"Yes, my dear, how do you come up with such recipes? I was supposed to taste each plate and take notes, and instead, I ate a plate from each."

"I close my eyes and cook, and I let my heart decide on the ingredients," I answered.

"But," he said, "there is a special ingredient I have never tasted before. Can you tell me what it is?"

"It is love," I said. "It is my lust for every meal and the passion I use while cooking. Love, lust, and passion."

He looked at me; his mustache was wiggling. "Are we still talking about food?" he asked.

"It is always about food—the way you handle it to the time you eat it," I replied.

He went on walking and laughing, saying out loud, "Love, lust, and passion."

He happened to be the oldest critic in New York. Robert said, "No restaurant survives without his consent. I guess we have to wait till tomorrow to read the review."

The atmosphere was beautiful; we truly put a great event together. Andrew had a close eye on the service and was walking around nonstop; Angela's voice traveled through the hills, entertaining the crowd.

Suddenly, she vanished, and the music stopped. We looked around and couldn't find her. "What happened?" Robert said.

"I don't know," I said.

Then I saw Lady running inside. "You have to take care of the situation and find a plan B," she said.

Robert looked at me and said, "You don't have to do it; you can simply add music in the background."

"It's about time I do what's best without pain," I said. I went to the microphone, signaled for the musicians to start, and began singing. The crowd went silent. I saw them freeze all actions, and the evening went on.

For one reason or another, I started with the song "Que Sera Sera." I had my eyes closed, and I was singing for Alisa.

While singing, I was talking to her. I was holding her hand and walking the meadows with her hand in hand, side by side.

I wish you were here, my love. Love you till eternity.

CHAPTER
FOURTEEN

"Cooked with love, lust, and passion—I wonder what it tastes like!"

The statement highlighted many papers the morning after the big day. I wished I was able to enjoy my success, but I was worried about Angela. All I knew was that she had gone back with Lady to New York without saying goodbye.

I spent the morning relaxing between the garden and Robert's private home. I did really feel at home. "Do you know anything about Angela?" I asked.

"Not really. I know there were people from the embassy of Africa, and they came late. Most likely, it is related to her past," Robert answered. "You know, Ale, if we do not reconcile with the past, it will come back to haunt us. I learned that the hard way. I want to share something with you, my Ale. When I was young, I was fascinated with speed. I ran over a guy in my car once. My dad used all his power to keep me out of jail, but he insisted on keeping me there for one night. He said if I didn't learn from my mistakes and see the other side of life, I would never learn. Luckily, the boy stayed alive, and after that, I went to pilot school.

"The family did not press any charges, because of my dad and his acts of kindness to the family before the accident and in the society. I guess when you do good to others, God sees your actions. I went to his family afterward and apologized, and the family became part of ours."

"What happened to the boy?" I asked.

"He is your assistant chef," Robert said. "We adopted his education, and he started working at the Hope Ranch. I have never forgiven myself, even till this day. Sometimes I have nightmares, and I thank God daily for his safety. Everyone has a story, and as long as we are blessed to survive it, life goes on. Which brings a point to the surface. I want to mention a point once and close the subject. Anytime you want us to get in touch with Alisa, you let me know. I will not act without your consent. And now we'll talk about your business."

"I love you, my man. Let things be now, and eventually, a day will come when I can speak about it freely and discuss different options. Anyway, I want to go back to see the shrink. What do you think?"

"Of course, my Ale. I will go with you and wait outside, and when you want me in, you tell me.

"Now, yesterday was a huge success. The intention of the event was to launch your catering services nationally. You have to read, my Ale, what they wrote about you; you will be proud of yourself. Lady, Mom, and I are at your service."

We were interrupted by the phone. His mom was asking to join us.

"Of course, my man. With pleasure," I said.

She came in with his dad, bringing a bottle of champagne. "Never too early for a toast," his father said.

"May I start?" I replied.

"By all means," his mother said. "It is your day and your time. Speak up, my dearest Ale."

"I want to toast to a wonderful family. You opened your heart to me before your home, and that alone means a lot to me. You reminded me of my family—the warmth, the love, the care. I truly thank you from the bottom of my heart."

"You are family, my dear," said the father. "We are happy Robert has for the first time allowed us into his personal life. We are proud of his choice. We appreciate genuine and hardworking ladies, and you remind me of my wife. There is a reporter wanting to interview you. Are you ready to launch your catering services officially? You have our full support, and it is yours, dear. It is your baby. What would you call it?"

"My baby," I said. "If it is okay with Lady, I would call it Alisa's Catering Services, but I will launch it in partnership with your family."

"Dear," said the father, "your baby can only be yours and yours alone. We have more than what we need; you deserve the gift of having your own baby, and by the way, Lady sends her blessing. You will be stationed in New York with her. We already discussed the expansion, and she welcomed the idea and said, 'Blessed be Alisa,' and you know what she meant."

Repetition of the word *baby* made me cry. Robert, knowing me, jumped and whispered in my ear, "Your secret is safe, my Ale."

I looked at him, shedding more tears. I hugged his mother and said, "Alisa is it. Alisa is my baby."

Being a woman and a mother, she cried with me. I remembered Robert's words about reconciling with the past, and I recalled being unfair to Georgia and Angela when they shared their lives with me while I reserved mine. I decided to have a fresh, clean start and hope for no judgment. I said, "I do have an Alisa."

"We know, dear," said both parents. "A successful café."

"No," I said while holding Robert's hand tightly. "I gave birth to a baby girl I gave up for adoption when I first moved from England, from a small town called Farmville."

"Oh dear," they said.

"Life has its own conditions. Let it decide what is best. We are sure you had your own reasons, but Farmville?" the mother said as Robert tried to change the subject. "Weren't you there, Robert, last week?"

Moments of silence took over the atmosphere. "Yes, I had a private trip for your friend, Dad." And he closed the subject.

Did Robert track my family? I thought to myself. *What are the odds? Why would he have a trip to Farmville?* I let it be, as the day was already overwhelming. I decided to see the reporter.

I got ready, we met, and we announced the launch of Alisa's Catering Services nationally, with the main office in New York. I was not ready to move uptown or leave Lady; after all, she was my guardian angel.

Hours later, Robert's mom told us that Georgia's surgery had been successful, and we needed to go see her. We all went, including Robert's father.

Georgia was wide awake. She was in pain but able to

talk. The doctor said, "We will remove the bandage in ten days. Georgia can move to the Hope Ranch for five weeks, where she should not be exposed to the sun. Then she will have another surgery in two months."

We were all excited, and we spent a great day. Robert's mother informed Georgia that she needed new uniforms for the workers, staff, and employees of the ranch. She told her she would have all her needs at her disposal, and Georgia could start as soon as she was ready. Georgia was in tears, thanking them. Georgia's mother couldn't say much; she was overwhelmed with the news.

There were still many stories to share among the ladies, but the environment was emotional, and nothing could be added at that time.

As Robert had said, everyone had a story, but what was theirs? I couldn't take more emotions that day, but opening up about Alisa had been the right thing to do. I felt better already, but it was time for a break. Shortly before sunset, I asked Robert to go on the boat.

We reached the boat. It was ready to sail, the crew were on board, and there it went. We anchored midocean, and we stayed up to watch the sunset, my favorite time of the day.

"My Ale, can you promise to stay with me?" he said. "I mean in your thoughts. Let this night be ours and ours only."

"Of course, my man. I am yours and yours only."

Silence was our companion, the moon was our guardian, and the wind was the only thing between us. Indeed, it was a night to remember. We embarked on a passionate night. No words were said; only the sound of our breathing floated in the air, and the boat rocked with our movement. *Can we ever have enough?* I wondered. *I guess when you love truly, you just can't have enough.* That was us more than ever, sinking in each other's sweat and ecstasy. With his fingers strolling down my body, my heartbeats were so loud I was able to hear them.

As for his lips, the only words he said were "Ale, my love forever," and other than that, they were all over me softly.

Love was not a memory, but being with Robert, I could not stop feeling him even hours after we separated. He was always in my thoughts. The time we spent together was so precious that I could not let go of it. *Is that true love, is it passion, or is it adoration? Does he feel the same about me? Does he feel me when not with me? Does he remember my touch? Obviously, I mean a lot to him, and he wants me continuously. Obviously, the feeling is mutual, but how far does he see us going?* It was a question I did not want to ask myself or him.

Hours later, I woke up on his shoulder, with him hugging me and deep asleep. I did not want to move or wake him up; I enjoyed listening to his heartbeat and translating the pulses of his heart into words I wanted to hear again and again. Shortly after, he woke up, and I wrote with my finger on his chest, "I heart you."

He smiled and kissed me on the forehead first and the side of my lips next. "I heart you more," he said.

"I need to see the shrink," I said. "I am ready to discuss Alisa with her. Can we do that before we go back to New York tonight?"

"Of course," he said.

"And probably later in the session, you can join," I said with a smile.

"Anytime, my Ale. I am yours and with you," he answered.

We spent the day sailing under the blue skies and away from all humans. I cleared my mind in the wind, and I threw all my concerns into the ocean. I needed to find peace within me, and I did. I guess Lady was right. *When the time comes, I will open up like a flower in the wilderness against all odds and will flourish against all beliefs. I believe when love knocks on our door, we just have to open it and let life take its course as naturally as it flows.*

That was the way I felt about love, and that was how I started my discussion with the shrink. "Love has taken me in different directions similar to a leaf in the wind. Sometimes it flew me right; other times it flew me left, and I just accepted love when it came and when it felt right. I always sensed it was meant to be and happen, but what is next with Robert? Is he for real? Is he going to step out of my life like many did before him?

"My parents let go of me because I was a dreamer. You cannot let go of your children if their dream does not come across yours. You cannot make them sleep because you are sleepy, and you cannot feed them when you are hungry; children are free souls, despite the bodies they grow in. They need to fly in order to know how far they can go. Yes, you raise them, give them the life skills they need to survive, and share your knowledge through experience for them to learn about what you did, but you are not raising, giving, and sharing with them for the purpose of their following your steps. Our duties as parents are to give unconditionally, support anytime, and nurture all along. Is that what my parents did? No. Instead, they were ashamed of my character and preferred I disappear. This is a sad statement but a true one. Regardless of the small-town gossip, the culture, the religion, the mentality, and all limits and red lines, if parents cannot accept their children, their character, and their dream, they should probably reconsider having children.

"Children are not a package you buy with a choice of instructions. Children are free souls. They came into this world as a result of an intimate moment to be loved, to mark their spots in life, and, hopefully, to make a difference in someone's life. Those are the children in my eyes, and those who cannot allow children to grow and be themselves and not a reflection of their parents should probably reconsider having children. That is how I feel about my parents.

"As for Alex, he was my first love and my first deception. He came into my life after I had lost faith in the beauty of life. I was still in Farmville, dreaming of leaving but with no plan. I was trying to compensate between school and work in order to raise enough money and fulfill my dream. I was a robot who was trying to smile. It is difficult for teenagers to struggle and understand the reason. That was where I was when Alex came into my life that night on the rock in my hometown. The time I spent with him was beautiful; till this day, I do not regret it. Not because of the outcome of our relationship but simply because I am someone who regrets nothing and considers every incident in life a step to the next level. Alex reconnected me with reality, but he was a very irresponsible man. Alex did not take charge of his actions, while I was a minor, a small-town girl, and I faced what I got myself into with great courage. My relationship with Alex resulted in a pregnancy, but he did not want the baby.

"However, what bothered me more than his not wanting the baby was how he disappeared and let go of me. With all the concerns a pregnant sixteen-year-old could have, well, I was wondering about true love. I realized then my strength. I started wondering about true love, and I decided, *I do not need a man in my life and never will.* After years of adjusting the puzzles of my life—because somehow, they never fell into place—I met Robert. Day one, I fell for him. Was I longing for such a man in my life? Many came before him who tried hitting on me and talking to me, but none made me feel anything until Robert. He whispered in my ear, and I still remember it till today.

"How come I allowed him into my life? How come I trusted him? How come I loved him?"

Although those sessions were meant for the clients to figure out the answers, the shrink couldn't help but say, "Robert is a genuine person. You need to trust your feelings at one point in life. You have most of the answers, and it seems to me that you always did. It seems you always reasoned everyone's actions, which defines your strength. You analyze reality faster than others. This is a good quality, but don't let your rationality stand in the way of your future. Robert is genuine. Love him back, and love him in return. Don't hold an umbrella while waiting for the rain to come. Enjoy the sunny days, and enjoy the rain.

"I am assuming you did the exercise I gave you on paper. Would you like to discuss anything else today?"

"Yes," I answered, "but I would like to add a guest to the session if that is fine with you." I called Robert in.

"Robert," she said with a smile.

"Julia," he said with hesitance.

"Oh, you two know each other?" I asked.

"He was my high school sweetheart. It never went beyond high school. Are you still comfortable?" Julia asked. "If not, I will transfer you to a colleague. I never knew which Robert we were talking about till today, so it's your decision, your call."

I decided to stay with her, but it took me minutes to gather my thoughts. "I would like now to discuss the baby I had. I want you to tell me about kids and what goes through the mind of an adopted child, assuming she is in good hands."

Julia started talking. Robert put his arm around my shoulders as we listened. I took my letter book out. Julia thought I was taking notes, but I was addressing Alisa.

Sweet Alisa,

Sweet daughter of mine, how I would have preferred to ask you that question in person. What is going through your mind right now?

I wish I could hear your voice. I have been missing you more and more every day—I guess because I have been talking about you more and sharing my love for you with those I trust and love. I know it is hard to believe my love for you, when I gave you away, but I believe that sometimes in life, we are forced into making unfortunate decisions. Always remember to trust your heart, and now your heart is telling you that I love you, because I am holding it with my hands and kissing you.

One day we shall hug for real.

Love you till eternity,

Your birth mom

CHAPTER FIFTEEN

Because of my personal journey, I'd learned to minimize questions to others, but Robert was not others. I knew that not asking Robert about Julia would end up building an obstacle between us. I always followed my intuition, and my intuition now was telling me to face the answers. *But do I want to know the truth? And what if he tells me there was nothing between them? Am I to believe him? Then again, if he says there was something, am I to believe it ended? Is this going to be a stumbling block between us?*

I had to make a decision quickly since we were in the car already, and it felt weird. We were both silent. We'd never before had that kind of silence, and it did not feel right. I was wearing a mask, hiding my true feelings, because I couldn't face my feelings. It was a beginning I did not like to have. I wanted honesty, I wanted continuity, and I did not want to change any characteristic in myself, except caring enough to ask and not fearing judgment. *If you love truly, you open all pages of your book—no secrets between the lines. That is what I did when I spoke about my journey while he remained silent. Why is it that he stuttered when he saw Julia, while she was professional enough to say, "Hello, Robert," calling him by his first name?*

My long rhetorical questions and one-sided conversation were interrupted.

"Julia and I were together till two years back, before you and I met," Robert said after he had taken an exit off the freeway and parked to the side. "I never knew you were seeing her, and I apologize for not telling you about her earlier. But when we met on the pier that night, I was no longer with her. I do not want her or any other incident to stand between us, and I want things clear between us. When you told me about Alex and Alisa, I felt my story with Julia was very lame in front of yours, and I truly wanted you to tell me everything about you, especially since you had opened up and trusted me. Additionally, it was a story long gone, and I had no more feelings toward her. I assure you that you are not a rebound person. My feelings toward you are true, and my intentions are sincere. Please ask me all you want, because I am not going back on the road till you say you want me to."

"Thank you, my love," I said. "I believe you." I did feel honesty in his words. "Everyone has a past. I want you to believe as well that my past ended in Farmville, and it no longer affects me—except for Alisa, of course. As for Alex, I never even think about him. I trust your words and hope you trust mine. Let us put the past behind us, and one day you will tell me about yours, because I would like to know all the details but not now."

"Love you, my Ale," he said, "and let us now enjoy the ride. I chose to drive because I want us to talk about the session with Julia, if you agree. If not, we'll talk about whatever makes you comfortable. When you asked me to join, I knew we had crossed a huge step. I do not want to rush anything, and I do not want to ruin what we have. Tell me, my Ale—what is on your mind?"

"Alisa," I said. "I asked about her because sometimes I consider having her back. I know it is not an easy process and would not be easy for her. And is it the right age to disturb her? But my main question is, does she know she was adopted? It's a question I ask myself constantly. I do not know where she is. While I know that Lady has all the details, I am lost and do not know whether I want to know. I need time to think without knowing where she is. I need to discuss all the pros and cons of reality before knowing where she is. And then, when the time comes, I will decide. Another very important point: Do I have the right to deprive a family who offered her all their love of a daughter they raised, just because now I've decided to have her back, especially after I requested full disconnection when I gave her away? Many questions go through my mind, to which I have no answers."

"Should I investigate?" Robert said. "Remember that I promised you not to interfere till I get a sign from you. Would you like me to gather information for you?"

"I prefer not, at least not yet," I said. "At this point, I'd like only the two of us to discuss things. When the time is right, I will go back to Julia and discuss my thoughts with Lady, because I know for a fact she has more answers than anyone. Now let us just go to the hotel and take care of business, especially seeing that Georgia is fine and well taken care of, and we need to check on Angela. Are you leaving soon, my man?"

"Thank you for your trust," Robert said. "The fact that

you would go back to Julia means a lot to me. It means you have faith in us, as I do, my Ale. As for going back to work, no, I am not at this phase. I am staying with you and focusing on launching Alisa's Catering Services. Additionally, we did not discuss the processed-food project yet."

"Do you think we will be stretching thin and might lose control over the operations?" I said.

"No, my Ale, the processed-food business will launch gradually in a department under my mother's supervision and your direction. That way, you will not have to leave New York City. But we need to discuss the details—what you want and what kind of products and market you are looking for."

"Robert, my love," I said, "that project was my first dream, and one of the conflicts with my parents was caused because of that project. We had a farm back home, and my parents used to sell dairy products locally, while my dream, starting in my early teen years, was to expand and sell to nearby cities. It would have been a huge success, especially as it would have been processed under a family business. Sadly, my parents could not see what I was seeing. To them, I was just a young girl talking and dreaming. So going into that business will be the launching of my first dream. Do you think we can accomplish such productivity?"

"Let me discuss it with my mom," he said. "We have the farm, the factory, you, and a great team. We'll need to expand and get professionals, my Ale. You need to know that this project is of great interest to my mom as well, and she will offer great support. What will you call it?" he asked with a smile.

"Farmville Products," I said. "What do you think? It was the title I wanted originally."

"I like it," he said, "and I am positive it will succeed."

The road trip passed in no time; we were both taken by the same interests. We reached the hotel, went up to the room, lay down on the bed, and took a long, much-needed nap. Our minds were more exhausted than our bodies; we needed to let go of all thoughts and emotions and relax. I was not ready to proceed to work till I saw Angela. I was worried about her.

Toward the afternoon, I called Angela, and Robert and I went to see her. Robert apologized for the awkward situation that had taken place at his house, and then he said he would wait outside while we talked, but Angela asked him to stay, saying, "I trust anyone Alexandra trusts."

Angela was no longer crying; instead, she was full of joy. We learned someone from the embassy had shaken her up. It was her first and only love. *It is always love*, I thought, *that shakes our ground and makes us flip, and this time, it was hers.* It was the story she never had finished when we were talking. No wonder Angela was so untouchable—no one interested her or caught her attention. While I thought she had her focus on her career and education, Angela was saturated. *What is the story of love? Why does it never come easily? Why does true love always have more complications? The harder the complications are, the deeper the love is.*

"After we moved to another state in Africa," she said, "I was enrolled in a new school, and being the new kid on the block, it was very difficult to fit in, especially because my political background news arrived before I did. I was never into politics; my dad never allowed me to take part. Although we had a youth club that was purely political, which included most of the politicians' children, in order to carry out the legacy of the parents, my dad wanted me to carry the legacy to a higher level. Partially, that is why I am studying political science but outside Africa. The school I attended was a private school, and only those who could afford it joined in.

"Amid my struggle to fit in, I met a student in high school, a lovely gentleman named Ronald. Everything about him was perfect, except his political affiliation. His dad was the opponent of my father politically, and accordingly, we were never allowed to be together. But as love is beyond all rules, I fell in love with him, and I emerged into a relationship—not only emotionally, but I joined his voice, which was a cry for freedom in Africa. I was convinced that was the right call. We cannot fight war with war. We were the new generation with a new frame of mind and a new voice. Our party was called the Voice of Freedom, and with a female as the vice president and Ronald as the president, we had a great charisma and started recruiting students, and many more joined from outside campus. Our Voice of Freedom grew, and no one could stop us. We both shared the same opinion: the need for a revolution but a peaceful one. That was not what we shared only; love united us before our common mission. We had our main office off campus, a place where our passion flourished.

"It was a small house by the lake where I was no longer a girl. One rainy night, I gave myself to him. The electricity was gone, the lake flooded, and no one was able to travel by land. So we stayed in after everyone was gone, and we lay by the fireplace, the only light we had. Between talking and hugging, I let myself go, and I spent the night of my life in the arms of the man I loved. I knew that night was going to change my life, yet I let go. The passion he showed me and that I showed in return made us realize we were meant for each other. Despite the cold, the heat of his breath warmed my soul, and I was like a heated lioness over her prey. I took it all with no regrets. That was one thing I learned from my dad: happiness comes with full determination. And at that moment, we were united; lust was our only focus, and I had no fear of tomorrow. I trusted his lips, his hands, and his passion. I trusted him. He was the man I wanted to deflower me; I wanted him to be my first and, hopefully, my last. I still remember that night, and till today, I still feel his breath all over me during my lonely nights. To me, I did it out of love, not under pressure. I was not raped like the many young girls coming to us for help. I was privileged to have found love and become a woman with my consent and with full passion. He was a man of my choice and a gentleman.

"The next morning, we woke up in each other's arms, but unfortunately, we were not alone. The army of my father and his guards were in the room, and the dreamy night woke up to terror. Luckily, they were taken by the passionate scenery and were not fighting. I covered my face with the blanket around us, and Ronald yelled at all of them like I never had heard him before. 'This is my woman you are looking at! Shame on all of you!' he said. I knew then that I was with a man way older than his age and a gentleman.

"They all left the room, waited for me to dress, and took me to my father. I reached home, and my mother received me on the street and took me from the back door to my room, where she asked me not to leave. She had my dad to deal with. The next day, I received my high school diploma with a ticket to New York City, and she escorted me to the airport with tears in her eyes. 'Till we meet again,' she said. She hugged me, and that was the last I heard from them.

"I dreamed about Ronald daily but never heard from him since, till the day of the event. Lady was trying to get us together, but she is still waiting for an answer from the embassy. I wonder whether he wants to see me, but I sure still love him and want to see him. Robert, can you help? Can you get me his news? Why is he here in New York?"

"He is the ambassador," Robert said. "I've met him a couple of times, but I have to say, he had a lady with him. However, he never introduced her. To be honest with you, she seemed more like a cultural attaché, not his companion, yet she is always with him. I will let you know and speak to Lady. I will leave you two now and come back in an hour."

It was the longest hour I'd spent. I was in bed, lying down with Angela, crying, laughing, and chatting. We spoke about love and how it changed us, and we laughed about the heated nights we could not forget.

Robert went out and had the common sense to call his father, and the first thing his father mentioned was a call from the African embassy asking about Angela. Robert took his number, and after discussing the outcome with Lady, he called Ronald and asked him to join. The lady with Ronald was a woman assigned by his father to ensure he did not play around and ruin his career.

There was a knock on the door. We opened it, and there he was. It was Ronald with Robert. He froze. Angela ran to him, they hugged, and love succeeded. He was still in love with Angela and had been looking for her. Robert hugged me and walked me out.

"Where are you going?" Ronald said.

"Down," Robert answered. "We will meet you in half an hour. We will all have lunch in the embassy."

Robert and I went to the lounge and sat there. Robert said, "Do you believe in fairy tales, my Ale?"

"Of course, my love," I said, and while waiting, I grabbed my letter book.

> Dear Alisa, sweet daughter of mine,
>
> Pure love shall always triumph; it shall never fail you. I hope one day ours will bring us back together. Learn to be patient, and learn to accept what love brings you. Your heart is the only mechanism that no one can beat, and love is the only tool that will set you free, despite the circumstances. I met a guy. He is not your biological father, but to me, he is the greatest father. He is helping me cope with us, and Robert says, "Send her my regards." He says hi to you. I hope you will get a chance to meet him. Who knows? Life is full of surprises, so let it be.
>
> Sweet Alisa, sweet daughter of mine, I'll love you till eternity.
>
> Your birth mom

CHAPTER SIXTEEN

It was just a matter of time before things started falling into place. Angela had found her love again, lunch at the embassy was excellent, and Robert and Ronald became good friends.

We started going out as couples, and our social network increased. The embassy adopted Alisa's Catering Services for all their events, and that alone kept me busy. The expansion at the hotel was ready within six months. Robert was supervising the construction, and he brought the assistant chef from uptown New York to help. Business was booming on all levels, except for Angela's, since Ronald did not want her to proceed in her singing career. We had to hire another singer, especially now that the hotel restaurant expected the entertainment service. Lady hired a pianist and a singer, and we launched a piano bar, which was a first in the area.

Creativity plays a big part in life, I thought, *and only those who dare heated situations shall live to see them bloom*. That was the story of each one of us, including Lady. She was not only a dreamer but also a gambler. That had been my opinion about her on day one on the deck of the boat when we first met. She'd bet on me, and together we'd succeeded. One needed to gamble to prosper. Although it required luck, having faith in self and the universe was a must.

Success was partly hard work but also required determination, the right people, and a heart to move on—qualities we all had, including Georgia. All of us had gone through trauma emotionally for us to be more focused on our careers. None of us let our love stand in the way of our future, but we all carried love along. I guessed love was a key element to success. I thought about those who built empires of success while they were still lonely. Whom would they share their success with? I believed that if you ended up alone, it meant you forgot yourself along the way. You forgot those who stood by you, supported you, and praised you. You let go of those who looked up to you.

I will not make this mistake, I thought. *I believe in the power of love, in two minds instead of one, in two hands to clap for success, and I believe in people. Time has taught me to find the best out of every situation and to find the good in every person around me, and with time, the universe will respond to my calls. As for those I saw the good in while they failed me, with time, they will live to regret the time they lost and the actions they took. I will not change for anyone. I will not waste my time on those who chose a path parallel to mine and away from me; instead, I will invest in those who joined me and had faith in me. This strategy has succeeded so far; it brought to surface the good people in my life. The puzzle of my life shall never be complete without Alisa at the heart of it, but*

I am still not convinced it is time to rock her world. It is a step I believe is not yet due. I will let the call come from her, from my daughter.

Among the twister of thoughts taking over my mind, I had to settle, and the only way was through cooking. I stepped into the kitchen, got the ingredients ready, and started making new dishes and sweets. I was not angry or lost; I simply had mixed emotions between reality and dreams. Too many things were happening all at once. Everything was looking positive, but still, I had a hollow spot in my mind that I could not control or fill. They were all talking and busy, and I looked at them, saying to myself, *I have to involve myself with this discussion. I am the key person to develop the project.* But I couldn't. It was too crowded. I couldn't even think.

Robert felt something was wrong, and he followed me to the kitchen with a three-olive martini. "Is my Ale okay?" he asked. "What is wrong, my love?"

"I just need to be alone for a while with you," I said.

He closed the kitchen door, put soft music on, took my hand, kissed it, twisted me, and started dancing. "Are things going too fast, my Ale?" he said.

"No, my love," I answered. "Just feeling a hole in my mind, despite everything."

"Are you worried? I do not want you to worry about anything. I am by your side and no longer leaving till all projects launch," he said.

"That is great news, my love," I said. "I simply need one favor: fill the hole in my head."

"There are two things that would make you comfortable," he said. "Hearing from your parents and Alisa, correct?"

"True, my love," I said. "I cannot get both off my mind,

as if they are calling me, but I do not want to take any step till I launch all."

"As you wish, my love," he said. "Tomorrow morning, we need to see the lawyer. He will come here. I want all businesses to be official. Are you ready for that?"

"Of course, my love," I answered while resting my head on his chest and dancing.

"Cheers to your future, to us, and to your peace of mind."

We were interrupted by his father. "So here is the party," he said, coming into the kitchen. He started twisting his wife, joining the dance floor, till he reached us. "May I have this dance with this beautiful lady?" he said. We exchanged partners, and his father looked at me and said with a reaffirming voice, "We are all in your support, Ale. Please be the strong woman we met, because you are a woman with solid roots, and I will not let anything put you down."

I smiled, and tears shed down my cheeks. "You remind me of my father," I said.

"Please let me be, with all due respect to him," he said, "till we all join this venture."

His words were soothing, reassuring, and different. Although Robert said them incessantly, hearing them from the head of the family felt different. I knew they loved me because they wanted what was best for Robert, but they also believed in me, and that was why they were offering me this business opportunity. They wouldn't have gotten that far if they had not believed in my potential. Anyway, I decided not to analyze but to go with the flow.

The next morning, the lawyer came and sat with me, Lady, Robert, and his parents. His father started the meeting by setting the points of all the deals, saying, "Alisa's

Catering Services will give full ownership to Alexandra, I will finance the expansion at Lady's restaurant, and the catering services will lease the location from Lady since it will be her ownership. As for Farmville Products, it will be owned forty-nine percent each by Robert and Ale, with two percent to the Hope Ranch."

"But, Dad," Robert said, "what about you and Mom?"

"Robert, my son, you are me and your mom, and you chose Ale. It is time you come back and join the family."

His mother said, "Nothing will make me happier than managing my kids' business."

I requested to speak and said, "I would like to put on record that I will give two percent of the catering services to the Hope Ranch." Lady was about to speak, but I interrupted. "You have given way too much, and it's time you just accept the deal."

Then his father said, "If we all agree, I would like the legal department to prepare the official documents. As for us, we need to celebrate. Ale, a full team will join you in the morning to discuss the products, the marketing, and the distribution; then you will have to be in the factory during the first week of production just to ensure things are as you wish them to be, and then you will come occasionally. When it comes to family business, we are a family, but business is business. We hold strong and manage properly, and the Hope Ranch will always be our family. Now, let's cheer!"

It was a busy morning but one I needed, and now, with everything clear, I still had one question that I kept to myself: *Will Farmville Products ever reach Farmville?* I decided to keep it personal, and anyway, at that stage, we were launching only nationally, not internationally.

The next few months were busy, and I barely had time

to think. Robert went back to flying but reduced the frequency. I did not want him to stop something he loved for anyone. Georgia had two more operations, and I had not seen her for three months, for it was an inner rehabilitation phase. Then, one day, I heard a voice behind me say, "I need to hire your catering services. What day is your next availability?"

I turned, and it was Georgia—a beautiful Georgia but a different Georgia.

"Oh my God, it is you! I miss you. I truly do. You look great." I jumped to hug her but then stopped myself. "Can I?" I asked.

"Fresh as new. Not to worry—I am very solid," she said. We hugged for minutes. "We have a lot to discuss," she said. "I was isolated for three months, and I was not even allowed to see my mom, but I do feel great."

"I will be done in an hour," I said. "Go get yourself comfortable, and I will see you shortly."

I was looking forward to seeing Georgia alone and talking to her heart-to-heart; out of respect to her sincerity, I owed her a lot. I wrapped up the day, and the timing was perfect, especially because Robert was on a flight overseas and Lady was traveling as well. We moved to the rooftop, a place we both needed. I ordered a bottle of wine, and we sat there calmly, away from it all.

For minutes, we were silent, enjoying the silence of the night, gazing at the stars, and once the wind kicked in, emotions surfaced, and words flew out of Georgia's mouth, expressing her gratitude, happiness, and inner peace.

"Where is Georgia? What did you do to her?" I said.

"Oh no, not to worry. She's still there, trying to keep herself out of trouble," she answered. "I almost had a relationship during rehab, and it was the only night they allowed me out for a tryout. Can't stay away from love, but at least this time, I did not get myself in trouble, or rather, I did not have time to get myself in trouble. I have changed. I will protect myself, I will appreciate myself, I will think highly of myself, and I will love myself. I will do so before expecting anyone else to do it for me. That is my main and only focus from now on.

"I cannot expect people to protect me when I throw myself of a cliff, I cannot expect others to appreciate me if I do not know my own value and set my own standards, and I cannot expect others to think highly of me if I am running too low and going out of my league. I will love myself first and last, and then I will show others how I expect to be loved.

"Ale, meet the new me. I know that accidents will happen, and I will have to face different challenges occasionally, but I know as well that no one will hurt me without my consent. People's problems are their own; they are not mine to solve. I will help them and try to change them but not on my counts. They will know now what I like, and I will ensure they know how to treat me. I will be easy on myself, I will do a lot to enjoy my time, and I will raise the bar of expectations when it comes to the people in my life.

"So this is the new me, the one I want your help in keeping. You accepted me in the past as is while you tried to get yourself in, and I always knew my behavior was against everybody's consent. You are a true friend, one who does not judge, criticize, or base her relationship on foolish moments.

"I want to apologize for the times when I made life difficult for you. I hope you accept my apology, because I know you are a friend for life, not a situational one.

"I do too, Georgia. Despite what you got yourself into,

I always admired your courage and thinking I was courageous. I believe luck played a big role in my life for me to fall around beautiful people. As for you, you fell, you stood, and now you are taking charge of your life. We are all different and unique in what we face and how we react. While you loved at the double, I trusted at the double. As you were slapped, I was, but in different ways. Before I moved to New York, I always dreamed of this future, though under different circumstances. But in my case, I had to leave. I got pregnant as a result of a passionate relationship that ended up being a slap in the face. We all get slapped once or twice, but when we don't learn from those two slaps, we will end up being slapped harder and harder.

"I do not want you to feel odd. We all have a story, and most importantly, I pray for us to learn our lesson very soon in life in order to enjoy the rest of it. No matter what we survive, we have to move on, we deserve to be happy, and we owe our happiness to ourselves. So if you are ready, it is my turn to request your help and support, because with all the beautiful things happening to me, I cannot find total happiness."

"Oh my dear, I am sorry you went through this alone, but you are young, and you will still replace your baby. You have a wonderful man by your side," Georgia said.

"I did have the baby; I did not abort her," I said. "She is alive and happy somewhere. Lady gave her away to a family who are taking good care of her and loving her as she deserves to be loved."

"My dear, where? Who?" asked Georgia.

I froze. "I don't know. I requested that the identity of the family remain anonymous." We both sat there silently, while in my heart, I wished Alisa were sitting with us.

I grabbed my letter book.

Dear Alisa, sweet daughter of mine,

Regret is standing in the way of my happiness. By now, you are almost twelve and going through puberty. An age when I wished I would be standing by you, offering my know-how. I don't know what to tell you, except that by your age, I was dreaming of leaving my hometown, Farmville, and moving to New York City. A dream way bigger than an adolescent, but I was determined to reach it, and I did. One day I will tell you about your biological father. I am sure you have many questions, and I owe it to you.

All I can tell you now is that your mom was a dreamer, her dream got her where she wanted, her passion got you into this world, and rationale took away from her the most precious thing she could ever have. She never knew the loss of that thing would stand between her and happiness, and that thing is you.

Love you till eternity,

Your birth mom

CHAPTER SEVENTEEN

Georgia and I spent a beautiful night. We rejuvenated our friendship, and she was as beautiful as ever. I always had admired her, a beautiful lady with a beautiful soul. Not many could see the beauty of others and dare to admire it; it took a pure soul to do so, and I knew I was one. I always managed to see the beauty in others, accept them as they were, and believe in their potential. Probably the source behind my success was the purity of my soul, and a big part came from my parents, not because they were Catholics but because they were believers. I believed that those who had faith in a holy power succeeded, and my parents, despite the fact that they were average financially, were rich in terms of faith. Despite their financial problems, they managed to help those in need as much as they were able and through the food they shared on the table. I still remembered the nights when we'd had hungry walk-ins at our dinner table. Both my parents believed in sharing and giving, and they fed walk-ins we never had met before and never saw after. I recalled my dad's words: "Share what you have, and God will give in return. It is called karma." Probably the karma of my parents had filtered down to my success, but where was Alisa?

"Alisa is her name," I told Georgia when she opened her eyes. "That is my sweet baby girl. She is somewhere. I hope she is happy, and I hope she is well loved. My book is almost fully open on the table today. Everyone knows about her now, except Angela; I did not get a chance yet to tell her. I want to be strong for Alisa, for the day I meet her. I want her to be proud of me and, hopefully, want me one day."

"Apples don't fall far from the tree," Georgia said. "I am sure she does. Move on with your plan, and let God handle the rest. Trust the future, trust yourself, and mainly, trust your heart. Do you know what I believe? I believe the wind carries our thoughts through the universe. I spoke to you intensively when I was in the hospital, asking for you not to change and to stand by me and accept me, and look at us—no change, as if we first met. You never changed, Ale. My thoughts were answered. Keep the beautiful thoughts; they will be answered."

With those beautiful words, we hugged and went down to my kitchen. Georgia decided to help till university started again and till her parents agreed on opening her tailoring shop. She was in her last year and was ready to launch her own line of clothing. She was taking charge of her life, and that was great news. I was proud of her.

Our lives were falling into place one piece after the other, including Angela's. Her love life was working as she wanted, and she was in her last year at university. Angela did not know that Georgia was back, so we had a surprise planned for the three of us. We called her over for lunch, and when she came, the table was set for three. She sat at the table and said, "I thought Robert was out of town."

"He is," I said, "and Lady is, but look who is joining us."

Georgia came out, and tears fell from happiness. "You are here, you are gorgeous, and you are healthy," Angela said.

"Yes, all is fine now, and I am fresh as new. We have a lot to discuss, and there is a lot I have to share with both of you," Georgia said.

We sat to eat. "I have a big problem," Angela said. "My parents called, and they want me to leave with them at the end of the term after my graduation."

"Great news," said Georgia. "Wasn't this your plan originally?"

"Not anymore. You missed a lot," said Angela. "My love came from Africa. He is the ambassador of Africa here in New York City, and my parents don't like him. He was the reason behind my being sent to New York City, and he is the man I dreamed of being with every night. Now he knows about the call and wants us to marry before they come."

"But," I said, "would you marry without their consent?"

"I will try not to," said Angela. "I had to convince Ronald to wait and meet with them on peaceful territory. I want them to meet the new him and get to know him, and then I'm hoping for positive results. I will not tell them about him till they come. I cannot even tell my mom, because all communications are bugged. My only hope is a miracle. Do you believe in miracles?"

"Well, I do," Georgia said. "Every day is a miracle. Believe it will happen."

Angela was shocked with Georgia's answer.

"Oh yes," I said, "meet the new Georgia." We all laughed and started filling each other in on missed news. We had a beautiful lunch and decided not to open closed graves.

All three of us had a lot to fill each other in on, including my telling Angela about Alisa. Now my case was at rest. Although Alisa was not with me, having friends was important, especially friends like mine.

We were sensitive when discussing love issues, since Angela's and my love lives were on track, and Georgia's wasn't, but the new Georgia saved the moment by saying, "Ladies, let me tell you one thing: I am becoming innersexual!"

"Is that a word?" Angela and I laughed.

"Yes," she said while tears rolled down her cheeks from laughter. "Yes, in my own dictionary, it means no one touches me but me."

Georgia was always the street-smart girl, and with her words, she broke the ice among us and begged us to share intimate stories, and shockingly, she discussed intimate moments as well but never past ones—rather, the ones she fantasized about.

We spent an erotic afternoon filled with laughter and imagination. I guessed life was back to normal, but this time, we took the excitement to a higher level.

What does the future hold for us? I asked myself while going in and out of the kitchen, preparing for the evening, and looking at the three of us. *Will there be love, passion, success, and adventures? Will we stay by each other?* They were questions I feared to wonder about, but at last, I truly felt a unity among the three of us that, for once, had everyone's consent.

I guess time will heal every wound, and strong women

will rise against all odds. That is the three of us. We lived the battles, but we rose through the fields.

Toward the evening, Andrew came, escorted by another young man. They joined us, but something was different. We hadn't seen Andrew for a while. He told us the big surprise: he'd decided to join a dancing team who were performing in New York City and were recruiting fresh young dancers. He'd auditioned that afternoon, and the results were to be posted the next morning.

I looked at him and said, feeling responsible since Lady was out of town, "Shouldn't you wait for Lady to come and then decide?"

He said, "Opportunities like this come barely once in a lifetime. It is one of the teams who come to New York City every five years. If I miss my chance this time, my age will not allow me to audition next time they come. If I get accepted, I won't leave before a month. Lady will be back in a week, and I will tell her, but of course, Ale"—he stood and put his arms around my shoulders—"you will have prepared her." And he left.

Why can't we have a normal day? I said to myself. *Why can't our lives be just like many other families'? Lady entrusted me with everything, but as well, she entrusted Andrew. I am not to blame.*

At the end of the day, Georgia said, "Dreams are there for us to follow. You helped him with being accepted by Lady, and it is time for you to help Lady accept reality. Dancers need to dance. Did you expect him to dance in school performances forever? Any team hiring him, or school, will be taking him on road trips."

"Georgia, my dear," I said, "you will never understand. I don't know how Lady will take the news."

The afternoon was still heated, when a surprise visitor

came in: a handsome, tall, slim, fit man with a bald head. "Greetings," he said.

I looked at him silently. I was speechless. I did not answer for seconds, and he gave another greeting. "Apologies," I answered. "Good evening, sir."

"The day is still young," he said. "Good afternoon. Is Lady here?"

I knew it was him. "No, sir, unfortunately, she is not. How may I help you?"

"She is still the owner, though, right?"

"Yes, yes," I said, stuttering. "I am the manager. She is out of town."

He smiled and said, "But I am here. Just tell her I passed by."

"And whom would I say you are?" I answered.

"Just tell her I passed by, and she will know." He left.

I ran after him. "Sir," I said, "will you come back?"

He smiled and left.

I stood there watching him leave. "Why did Lady have to be out of town now?" I said loudly.

The girls looked at me, and Georgia said, "Are you okay? What happened to you? Why did you stutter? Did you see your face?"

I answered, "You haven't felt my heart." *A handsome man, Lady, my dearest. No wonder you are still missing him*, I told myself. But I was saved by a busy evening that took my mind off the heated events of the day.

It was too much for me to handle in one day. I did not know which news I should start with when seeing Lady: Andrew or her dream man. I couldn't sleep. Although the hotel was packed, I was all alone. My mind was more stressed than my body.

I started wondering whether he was coming back for

Lady, Andrew, or the hotel, but Lady had said the hotel was hers now. *So he must be coming for either her or Andrew, but he did not ask about his son. Is he coming to break Lady's heart again? She doesn't need any headache. She deserves to be happy. She is accepting her life. What gives him the right to step in at his convenience and rock her life?*

I never had been good at understanding men. They got a chance to be with the perfect woman, and they blew it. Did they rationalize that their dreams were more important than the person by their side? Were they satisfied with an ongoing trip alone, or once they were close to the end, did they come back? *Is that why he is here? Is he near retirement, and he came back to gain the only heart who loved him? Why do they take the only woman who loves them truly for granted and expect her to jump at their call?*

I might have been jumping to conclusions, but I was blessed with the sense of reading people's minds, and the way he'd busted in, he'd seemed to be expecting a big welcome.

Is Lady taking him back? Should Lady take him back? Well, I feel her dilemma already. Is there ego when it comes to love?

Love, the story of many generations—what can we teach our kids if we never master the basic skills? We hear many stories, but they all fall into the same trap: "What if?"

This gentleman had come in feeling sure that Lady was still available—how cocky was that? He took her love for granted across many years. She must have expected him to bust in the way he did many times, but he never did; he was too busy with his own life. Finally, he came, sure she would be there. Well, what if she had remarried—a beautiful lady like her? What if she had hooked up with another man? But what if she still loved him?

I wished there were a handbook of love that started with friendship rules and ended with love rules. *Would we disregard it, fall in love, and hurt ourselves and others? Does love hurt? Do men understand the concept of pain when they drop the flag of love and say, "I am done," and move on, and do they realize what they leave behind? Do men have any second thoughts when they leave a woman with a child behind to go follow their dream? Do men have regrets? Do men ever grow up?*

The same questions applied to women when they turned their back and lived with no regrets, but how many women turned their backs for no return, especially when there were children involved? *Wait. But I did. I let go of a very precious love and jewel, my child, my own, so I am not any better than this gentleman. He let go of his son, and I let go of my daughter. He followed his dream, and I followed my dream. He came back for his love. I will never go back to Alex. Andrew's father never asked about his son, and I never ask about my daughter. So I was right when I asked Lady if I reminded her of Andrew's father, but she said no, I am nothing like him; I am a totally different situation. And going back in time, I know I never wanted to marry Alex. I never wanted to settle far from reaching my dream.*

The resemblance was there in human nature, male or female, when we put our own personal interest before the interest of those who counted on us. Whether they were counting on our love or responsibility, I believed that our dreams should include the people who shared them with us. *We cannot just drop the flag of love or responsibility when our plans change*, I thought. *Well, that is life, and we are only human, far from being perfect.*

The sun was about to rise. While I was still turning in bed from one side to the other, I grabbed my letter book.

Dear Alisa,

After a long night, I tell you this: perfection in your eyes is different from perfection as seen in the eyes of others. I cannot ask you to be perfect while my mistakes increase with my age. My advice to you out of love is to live with love and to love with passion. No matter what you do, how cautious you are, and how considerate you might be, one day you will end up hurting the person who loves you the most, accepts you as is, and wants to be with you unconditionally. I guess life has no rules and none to be considered by the book, at least not mine. I wish I could tell you otherwise, but simply, be happy.

Love you till eternity,

Your birth mom

CHAPTER EIGHTEEN

I had more questions surrounding me than answers and more worries than reassurances. Although Robert and his dad were offering me security in terms of the business and all developments, including my rights, which were protected, with time, amid the view of the different situations around me, I forgot to heal the doubter inside myself. It all went back to the day my parents pulled their hands away from mine.

I believed we, as humans, were the product of the situations we survived. We might move on with our lives and heal our physical wounds, but we carried the scars that once blemished our soul with us to the grave. We pretended they no longer existed, but they always held us back. They popped up in different situations, strangled our decisions, and made us wonder about continuity.

Young adulthood was a crucial time. Those who were abused would never trust again. Whether male or female, they would hold back in every relationship, and that was

Georgia's case. I did not blame her for turning innersexual. Georgia was an outgoing girl who was manned by her heart, followed her instincts, and went with the flow. Her guts led her to undesirable circumstances. She tried to let herself be the changing agent in the couple, but she was trapped between love and abuse. She thought she could change the abuser, but she ignored the fact that abusers had many personalities, swayed between emotions, and distracted victims to a point where they could no longer see right from wrong. Victims became slaves to that love in the relationship, and till they were totally hurt, they still believed they could help the abuser. While subjected to pain, which they believed was love and were convinced was love, they pretended they were in control of the situation. They had make-up sex that was tender and sweet; faced unbalanced treatment by the abuser that went to both extremes, from wonderful to disastrous; and were showered with gifts by the abuser, and they became totally lost. During that phase, they rejected every bit of advice and pulled away from those who pointed at the abuse in their relationship, their best friends. The abuser then isolated the victim, and the victim became more and more under his control.

At that phase, fear took over the victims. They became sedated, and they started losing weight or gaining weight; they lost life perspective; and their facial expressions became still, as if they were in a coma. They pretended to have continuity, but in reality, they were no longer alive. It was a damaging phase for victims; they were eaten by fear when alone and in the presence of the abuser. Isolation became their remedy; loneliness became their best friend. They faced sleepless nights, and when they slept, they were woken up by nightmares. It was a cycle, especially when the abuser became more dominant and more attached to them, a theory the victim translated into jealousy and love. After that, the victims tried to socialize and deny the abuse, but the shame of admitting the abuse and the shame of the pain stood between them and their friends. If someone broke their trust and interfered to help, they shut them out, and they did so while pretending all was under their control. That was the cycle of abuse. Victims might be sexually abused, physically beaten, burned with a cigarette, pushed in public, slapped, or end up with a brain concussion, broken ribs, and bruises.

Many lived in fear, were ashamed to admit the pain, and isolated themselves. I wanted to tell them all, "You cannot break the circle of abuse alone. Get help. You will never be judged, but you need to be protected. Abusers are sick, and they need help. If you think you alone are living in shame, try being the abusers with fingers pointing at them as mentally sick. Try being the abusers and living with their conscience. Try sleeping at night while worried about the news of paying the price. Karma is on your side, and loved ones will always be there for you. Get yourself out, protect yourself, and speak out. You are not alone, and you will never be judged. Do it today. You are precious, and no one has the right to make you feel any less."

Abuse was one phase a young adult might survive. There were many of them, including being betrayed. That was the case of Angela. Angela was betrayed by her parents. Her love relationship was judged by her parents, and they sent her to another country, disregarding her feelings, the outcome of the travel arrangements, and the host country. No wonder Angela limited her life to studying and singing. Her father's choice to exile her was purely ego-centered. She could not understand as a young adult, or at any age, why her right to love Ronald was denied, especially since the movement she had launched with Ronald was the beginning of a peaceful campaign well due. Peace was overdue in Africa; it was needed for the upcoming generations to live in serenity. However, her father's beliefs and political affiliation were jeopardized. But how much trust should the father have had in the system that betrayed him personally and on a family level? The system he was connected to had betrayed him and could not protect him; he'd had to leave his home, town, and friends and relocate to another area. The system could not even keep his home and protect his life treasures; not only did he have to relocate with his family, but his home became a fort for the opponent. Why trust those who could not protect your treasures? Although he was offered full immunity, losing memories and the past was not the perfect solution for a family. His wife and daughter supported his situation willingly, but in time, he forgot those who stood by him out of love and not out of duty.

As for the love situation, Angela was betrayed by her own dad, who assumed her love relationship was an opposition to his priorities. His priorities were focused on what was best for his political affiliation, while he forgot his main and initial unit, his family. He did not even see Angela after the incident. Was he ashamed of Angela's love relationship, or was he more ashamed of the person she fell for?

I wished I could ask every dad, "What is more important to you: your family and children or work? Will you be satisfied if your own daughter feels you pulled away from her the hand that was the most important to her security? How do you expect her to trust the community she lives in after being betrayed by her own main nest?" My last question was to Angela's dad: "Are you coming to the graduation, a very important day for your daughter? Why do you want her back now? Is it because you know Ronald is in New York or, again, because her life is your choice, and you manipulate it at your convenience?" Angela's dad, like many others, thought about what was best for him. Unfortunately, Angela's mom was another betrayal story; she could not face the man of the house and, in turn, protect her children. I wanted to say to both parents, "Do you know what you make of your children when you betray their trust? Do you know the fearful monster that inhibits them when they are outside their safety nest? Hold on to your children's dreams, even to what is, in your opinion, a mistake. Keep them under your wings, because in Angela's case, you were lucky she did not revolt to undesirable flames."

The only remedy to deception was heat. It could be love, including wrong love; drugs or alcohol; foolish outings; or inappropriate friends. Luckily, Angela reserved herself—and not for her parents. She was loyal to the love she believed in, and she was lucky to cross paths with that love again.

The best example of deceptive love was Lady's. Although rejected by her parents for being pregnant, she found security with her passionate man. But at times, if we were committed to deception, we attracted it through our choices. Lady was so in love with Andrew's father that she decided to keep the baby out of love for the father and his child. At least in her case, Andrew's dad offered her all the security she needed to survive with the baby. Did he ever come back for her? No, not until now, but she was determined to move on with her life with Andrew and make the best of it by being a successful woman. She made it and raised the bar of her hotel, which was the first in the area manned by a woman. Did Lady not love again—a beautiful woman like her? Did not many men want her, or did the rejection from her parents and then Andrew's dad make her keep her hand in her pocket and not give it to any other man? Or did her success on her own make her self-satisfied and in no need for a man? Was financial security important? Of course, but did it stand in the way of marriage and company if the woman was well established? Was that Andrew's dad's plan: to give enough for Lady not to consider another man? Was love not needed when financially secure? Well, that was not what Lady had advised me to do. She'd encouraged me to love and live but with restrictions. She had pushed me toward Robert but only Robert, not the other acquaintances I had. Was it because he was a gentleman and a well-off man, or had she developed with time enough maturity to know who was a keeper?

Another young adult who was deceived was Andrew. I truly wanted to know all about him because he was my Alisa. How did a child feel when he knew he was not wanted by one of his parents? How did he react to family, love, companionship, self-esteem, trust, loyalty, and faith? Andrew suffered the absence of a father as he was growing, and Lady, while knowing his artistic interest, denied it, fearing he would follow in his dad's footsteps and not wanting to remember his dad. Both parents showed self-centered and egoistic trends. As a mom, Lady could not protect him while he was bullied for his interests, and she let him stand alone. She was not wrong, but it was not the right thing to do. Andrew's inclinations could have been genetic or intrinsic actions toward the solitude he survived, the absence of the father, and the ignorance of the father's identity. I felt that wondering about one's roots was a solid step toward security. Although Lady tried to secure all Andrew's needs, she failed to fill one gap, a question I was sure he sought the answer for: the identity of his father.

Andrew mentioned to me at one point his interest to know his father and about him, but he said that out of care for his mom, he didn't ask. Did lady know that? I never told her. And did Alisa want to know about her parents? Andrew had one parent who did not want him, but in the case of Alisa, both parents did not want her. I gave her away while thinking it would be best for her to have a full family who loved her and not only one parent, but I never took into consideration the way she might feel about it one day. When I asked Andrew about his father, his answer was "I'd prefer to know his identity rather than wondering who he is, and I'd prefer to know how much of a selfish person he is rather than my judging him." In my case, I asked for Alisa to know she was adopted. Was it the right thing to do? With as little as I knew back then, I thought it was her right to know.

My life since Farmville had been full of deceptions. After my sister was sold to her husband, I felt a lack of trust in my parents. I was too young to act and afraid of the moment the same decision reached me. I decided to work. What was wrong with entertaining in order to raise money? I believed people could keep their respect in whatever careers they were in. A woman could be harassed if working in a factory, at a school, or at a restaurant and while being a waitress or an entertainer. It was not up to the community to decide on one's career and definitely not up to the parents to stand in the way of a child's dream. I merged my dream with theirs, but unfortunately, they wouldn't develop what they had. They did not trust my dream. While I offered them a secure development, I was still a teenager. My parents never knew about Alisa. I left before they knew. The singing career I chose at that time was enough for them to wrap my clothes in a blanket. How could I forget the silent statement saying, "You are no longer our child"? How could I ignore the feeling I had when I had to leave the house or let go of my dream? A child's dream was part of his or her future, and the support of the parents for the dream was the pillar of his or her future. Boys or girls, they were all alike; they deserved the same chances and the same support. One who felt deception in the nest would live with uncertainty in the world.

That was my case; nevertheless, I was blessed to meet Lady. Lady offered me the love, care, and support I'd dreamed of having from my parents. I had paid her back in services and the development of Lady's Hotel. I knew it would never be enough, but she was not expecting anything in return; she truly wanted what was best for me.

Life, what do you want from us, and what do we expect from you? It was a question every individual asked. I knew that the most important thing was not to carry the debris of the past along to the future. Not only would it delay us, but it would stand in the way of our development. The past was the pillar of the future. It was filled with lessons we should benefit from, and I believed we should forgive or, rather, accept people's actions toward us, for they didn't know any better. If they knew better, they should help themselves, because a day would come when they would look in the mirror and deny what they had done to others, but when they looked into their hearts, they would live to regret the loss of those they'd wronged.

Oh dear, I truly need to see Julia. One reason, in

addition to many others, was to face the only person I knew of who could stand between me and Robert. I did trust Robert, but my instincts told me to face my fear. I thought, *I will not move on with my life with Robert with any doubts. I will talk to her woman to woman, and she will know that Robert chose to be with me, as I chose to be with him. I will not avoid her; instead, I will keep her within my field of vision, and who knows? Being me, I truly believe she could be a good friend, with limitations, till further notice.*

I grabbed my letter book.

> Dear Alisa, sweet daughter of mine,
>
> Our choices in life are limited to the day we can take responsibility for our own life. Don't fear asking the questions that put your future on a smooth path. The day we were born is the day our journey started. Yes, I did give you up for adoption, but this is your fate; your destiny is what you make of your life. At your age, I left home while I was pregnant with you. I went to face the unknown, not knowing what my future held for me, but I had full faith in my potential.
>
> Believe in yourself, and life will believe in you.
>
> Love you till eternity,
>
> Your birth mom

CHAPTER NINETEEN

Somewhere along our journeys, we all had to talk to our past. We all wondered about different times, different situations, and different reactions that led us to where we were. There were things that were givens in life, those we were born with, such as our parents, name, background, and religion and many others, but our choices and reactions made the day, and unfortunately, we could not go back and change them.

Life was an equation of events. You could add, multiply, divide, and deduct different emotions, people, and locations, and the result would be what you had and what you were. It was easy to say but not easy to apply, because there was no way back. There was no rewind or pause mode in life; you had to just keep on going.

Choices were what made our future, and I had learned not to regret any but to empower my future based on the lessons I mastered. From deceptions to doubts to truthfulness to reassurances, I learned to be cautious. I learned that love was a must, and if I didn't love myself, I would never be able to expect love back or spread my love. That was the only thing I could never hold myself from doing, and I was blessed with love in return.

Although I was disappointed with Alex, who broke my heart with his reaction to my pregnancy news and his disappearance, anyone not willing to take charge of his actions was not worth being in my life. I knew I was not ready for marriage anyway. Alex was a great lover but not even half the man I'd expected him to be. When he moved on with his life, he proved he was not worth my thoughts and not worth my time. He was another shock to me; he was pure disappointment in manhood.

Alex was not my first disappointment; my parents were the big bouquet. How could one expect a teenager to fight for her dream when she lost the power of the nest? Well, I did, because the inner strength I had was sturdier than the events flashing my way. *Should I thank both my parents and Alex for what they have taught me?* I wondered. *Did any of them expect me to crawl back for forgiveness?* They'd helped to form the way I thought: *Always move forward. Whoever let go of you once will let go of you again and again.* That was a policy I followed, and I was proud of myself for going through with my life without looking back. I would keep the looking back for those who hurt me, ignored me, and let go of me. I was sure they did look back but was not sure how much.

If I could have sent them one message, it would have been this: "I did succeed on my own. I may not be proud of all my decisions, but I did the best I knew how." The sentiment was mostly about Alisa. I never wanted to cause her any pain. There were justifications for my actions, but when one felt she could not offer the best others deserved, plan B was due, and that, to me, was enough of a justification. At the time when I had Alisa, I was barely able to take charge of myself, despite Lady's support. I had to offer Lady a lot in return for what she offered me, and by doing so, with the late and long hours I spent in the hotel and the courses I took, I would have neglected Alisa, and neglected children were lost. Many might have disagreed with my decision, but it was mine only—mine to regret and mine to feel its pain. I would miss her every moment I lived.

Years had passed, and everyone had changed, including me, but nothing would change the way I felt about the past, betrayal, disappointment, and deception. That was the way I wrapped it up.

A couple of days after the stranger stepped into Lady's Hotel, Lady came back from her trip, a trip like many others: fully discreet in terms of the location and the reason behind it. Out of respect for her privacy, I never asked the reason, but deep in my heart, I hoped she had someone to love her the way she deserved to be loved. I felt sure she had love somewhere, especially with all the love she had to offer. After I summarized to her what had happened during her absence, I told her about the gentleman and his message. She was thrilled with all the news till the bit related to him, and then she asked me to leave her alone, something she had not done before. I did leave her alone. I took care of the restaurant. Then I decided she had been alone throughout her life, and it was enough, so I got us two glasses of Martini with three olives and went up to her.

I knocked on the door and went in. Lady was in tears, going through a memory box. "The past will always knock on our door unexpectedly," I said while giving her the Martini glass.

"Does he still look good?" she said with tears rolling down her cheeks.

"He doesn't deserve your tears," I said, "but yes, he does, and I knew it was him. Andrew is a replica of him. Andrew had just left when he came in. I don't know whether those are tears of joy for him to have stopped by or tears of desolation for missing him."

She said, "I knew he was coming to town, but it has been a while since he stopped by. Last time, Andrew was five."

"Speaking of Andrew," I said.

She looked at me with despair, saying, "What else is there to know?"

"He auditioned for an international dance troupe," I said. "He was supposed to get the answer by now, and he asked me to prepare you."

She laughed and said, "Well, the shock is in someone else's court now. Sarcasm of destiny. Any other news?"

"No," I said, "the rest is good news. I thought you would be happy to know he came looking for you."

"Ale, my love," she said, "life taught me to be the woman every man wants, not to be the woman wanting a specific man. As for Andrew, I did the best I knew how in terms of raising him and trying to keep him protected from a man, his father, who might ask about him every five years when in New York City, if convenient to his schedule. As for Andrew's dad, I wish I could have been a fly on the wall when someone carrying his exact name and looking exactly like him auditioned to join his troupe. You know the last decision is his in terms of accepting new members, but how would he justify the name, the resemblance, and the decision, knowing the inherited talent of Andrew? Andrew is mature enough to know the truth now, but I wonder if his dad is mature enough to take on a responsibility he denied years ago. I believe it is time to have the talk with Andrew. Do you mind calling him?"

"I did already, upon his request," I said, "and he's already on his way, but I did not ask about the results of his audition."

Shortly after, Andrew came in.

"Do you want me to pack the box?" I said.

"No, my dear," she replied. "It is time for Andrew to come up to the top floor."

Andrew came in, but Lady had no power to stand. "Sit near me, my love," she said after he kissed her.

"I will leave you alone," I said.

"No, my Ale, sit and learn. An experiment you shall go through very soon," she said. "Just order us a bottle of champagne. I have a feeling it is a celebration night."

"So you know?" Andrew said. "And you approve? Because I did audition without your knowledge, but I prefer to go with your blessings and consent."

"Congratulations, my love. I knew this day was coming. It is in your genes. But tell me all about it from day one," Lady said, "and feel free to skip the school days."

Andrew was thrilled, full of emotions, and said, "I auditioned ten days ago. I danced to a very special song, 'Que Sera Sera,' inspired by your singing, Ale. Everyone clapped and stood when I finished, and then this arrogant gentleman stood and said, 'No decision is final till we meet.' I came rushing to Ale and told her, and then a couple days after, I received a call. It was a lady, and she said the decision was not final, but I was asked to go again for an interview and a step-up, since the final decision went to the main owner and director, who failed to see some of the steps. 'But you all clapped,' I said, and she answered,

'I apologize, but the owner and director insists on seeing you one more time.'

"I went to the second audition, and the arrogant man was there, sitting in the dark, while all others were there in the light. They had a set of questions about where I'd learned to dance this way and about my parents, my education, and, specifically, my dad. I told them how I developed my skills alone, how I was bullied for my artistic choices throughout my school years, and how I knew nothing about my dad, but I'd dedicated my dance to my dad during the first audition. The arrogant man was throughout in the darkness and never spoke. Then he gave them a piece of paper, and I saw his hand. Then the lady said, 'We will put on a song for you, and we need to see you stepping up. Can you do so? It is called "My Dad," by Paul Petersen. Would you like to hear it once before you start?'

"'I prefer to do so, if you don't mind,' I said, and the music started. It was a very emotional song. I believe the choice was based on my story about my dad. I heard half the song, and it brought many questions to the surface. Would I ever have sung such a song to my dad if I had known him? Anyway, I thought they wanted to see me perform in an emotional state. I did, and again, they all clapped at the end of my performance, but this time, the clapping started with the arrogant man. Then he passed another paper to the lady, and she said, 'Congratulations. You have just been accepted, and we need to see you for training daily from ten to four while preparing your contract.'"

"Did you sign the contract?" Lady said.

"Not yet," Andrew answered. "I will be signing it with the owner and director at the end of the week, but I have received one-on-one training with him daily. He is a great dancer and choreographer. I am so happy."

"What is his name?" Lady said.

"We all call him Andy," Andrew answered.

"Andrew, my love, let's toast to your success. You are a natural-born dancer," said Lady. "Despite my attempt to stand between you and your artistic genes or to look in different directions and ignore your genes and talent, you made it. Cheers to your future and to destiny. Fate took away your father, but through what you made of your destiny, you succeeded.

"Your father never knew whether the baby I had was a boy or a girl. He left to pursue his dream and did not want us to interfere with his future. That is why I never opened his subject. He thought that by securing our future financially, he could free himself from any responsibilities; therefore, he transferred his hotel into my name. Keeping his identity and all related information in the dark was my decision. It might have been the wrong decision, but you were my focus, not him. I did not want someone who might deceive you with his selfishness to give you the shock of your life. Andrew, my love, this is a picture of your dad." She handed him a picture. "The universe plays in mysterious ways."

"But this is Andy," Andrew said.

"Sure is," she said. "Andy is your father. I named you after him, hoping that would be an additional reason for your paths to cross one day, under the same name, although every time I called your name, I remembered him.

"I will give you one piece of advice: don't let the past stand in the way of your future and your rights. Your father was young, selfish, and foolish, but he has wised up, from what I have heard from you, to give both of you a chance to get to know each other and let the days approve or reject your relationship. You deserve to get to know your father and, although I hate to say it, give him a chance to get to know you. The universe united you. Let it be, but lower your expectations, and then whatever he offers will be a plus. Always remember that you joined the dance troupe before knowing you were joining him. Enjoy your life and your partnership. Nothing competes with a partnership between father and son."

Andrew's day was happily messed up. No words could have described his feelings. He was lost and did not know whether he should be happy or sad. He sat there silently, listening to Lady, but most of her words were just humming to his ears. After a couple of hours, he spoke. Lady and I knew he was in shock, and he said, "Please, if you ever see Andy again, do not tell him I know who he is." Then he left.

I had learned in life that things came in packages. Whether joys or sorrows, they always came in packages, and everything had a price. Occasionally, it was money, but most commonly, it was more precious, such as time, friends, and family. That was why I had learned to hold on to what I had, accept losses without dramatizing, and grab the damages lightly toward the future.

Forgetting the past was a lie; forgiving was an untruthful act; and pretending to be fine while stabbed, ignored, rejected, or deceived was a misleading reality. No one could ever heal from a pain once felt and a scar once marked, whether physical or emotional. The difference was in the way each individual reacted to physical and emotional pain. Some accepted what they lived, claiming it was their fate; others took it as a challenge and decided to beat it; and some used physical and emotional pain to change their destiny. I fit into the last category. I would not accept being dragged down or held back. It might, at times, take time for me to rise, because I was an emotional and sensitive person, but I would rise again and again.

I was not worried about Andrew; one who was able to rise among nasty childhood friends, develop his talent alone to reach professional levels, and reserve a strenuous spirit, in my opinion, was one we should respect and learn from. Andrew had proven to all of us around him his loyalty, maturity, and determination, and having someone with those qualities around was a blessing. I hoped he would not fall under the trap of anger and lose what was best for him. He deserved happiness, but what was happiness, after all?

The day was too emotional for me, and I was not yet able to absorb the words Lady had said earlier: "Sit and learn. An experiment you shall go through very soon." So I grabbed my letter book.

> Dear Alisa, sweet daughter of mine,
>
> I truly hope you are surrounded by people like Andrew, who is a perfect example of determination to succeed, and additionally, I hope there is someone in your life like Lady, who would advise you to accept the parents who once let go of you. I wish many things, but to be honest with you, I truly wish I was hugging you right now.
>
> Love you till eternity,
>
> Your birth mom

CHAPTER TWENTY

Happiness is where the heart is, heart is where home is, and home is where the family is. So where is my home? Where is my family? No wonder my happiness is uncertain.

I was stretched between the past and the present, and no matter how much I pushed myself to move on, I missed my family and regretted that I never got their blessing. I understood Andrew's meaning when he'd told Lady, "But I prefer to go with your blessings and consent." They were golden words, I believed. I kept myself busy, ignoring the past, but in reality, I missed them and felt it probably was time to reconcile with the past.

Meanwhile, the food-processing production launched successfully, and within months, the distribution covered all states. I visited the factory every week, and we expanded to the production of all dairy products and started making fruit-and-yogurt snacks, which were welcomed heartedly. Robert was in charge of the marketing and distribution, and I stopped following on the location. I knew only that billboards carried the brand in all states, and the expansion of the factory was ongoing.

I guessed my initial idea was a successful one. Oh, how I would have loved to have my parents be proud of me. I knew that in due time, they would be, but would they like to hear about my success? Would they ever want to see me, forget the past, and forgive my choices? I would leave it to time and let things be for now. Anyway, with the hotel, the catering service, and the production, I was fully involved, and too many things were on my mind other than my work. I had Andrew to follow up on, Georgia's progress to monitor, and Angela's parents to deal with.

Georgia was still helping in everything and was around us at all times; she even had moved to the hotel. However, she never slept in the room alone, and when I was away at the factory, she slept in Lady's room. We all understood her fear of being alone and accepted the fact that she needed time to feel secure again. "Sometimes I wish I was still in the hospital," she said nonstop. But pain was relevant to the mind, and fear was a stage people overcame when they felt secure. Georgia had recovered physically, but emotionally, the scars were deep, and only love could heal. But she was not giving herself a chance to move on, and no one could push her to do so. Her comfort zone was among us, and till she was ready, we would not let go of her.

Andrew followed Lady's advice and remained with Andy's group, but he told his dad when he faced him that he was there because of his potential and not for being his son. His statement proved his maturity and strong personality. He shocked us all. He requested to be considered a student and to keep the relationship between them professional till he decided to take it to the next level. Within no time, he performed within the first row. After all, apples didn't fall far from the tree, and he showed great talent onstage.

We attended every performance in New York City, and when Andy came to see Lady again, her answer was "It is not my turn, and I have no other words to say." It was a strong statement that was said but not meant. It was tough to say to the love of her life, especially when she still had feelings for that person. Lady had expected him many times throughout the twenty-something years and wanted him to come back but not at the cost of Andrew. Andrew's reconciliation with the past and his dad was her priority, and despite the fact that she might lose him forever this time, Andrew was her main concern. Lady proved to be a strong lady. She was a role model for all of us in the younger generation, but deep inside, I felt her pain, I felt her agony, and I saw the tears she wept in her heart.

If love is a driving force to success, what about lost love? I wondered. *How can someone survive when the driving force is disabled and taken away? Who will take care of us, wipe our tears, and be the loving shoulder when one is needed? How did Lady survive all these years while her heart was still hanging, and she knew it was rejected?*

Lady did not allow any opportunity to knock on her door. She faced her fate with a Martini glass on the rooftop of the hotel, and instead of allowing love into her life, she offered love to the extent of recuperating for her own. She used the love she offered to others as a remedy for her deception, and I was the one receiving that love. Lady used her love for Andy as the generator of her success; she set aside what he had done and kept in her heart the good memories.

It was a lesson I learned from her and applied on a daily

basis. I guessed that was where my strength came from. The years I'd lived with Lady now equaled the number of years I'd lived with my family. When they'd closed a door on me, she'd opened her heart for me, and that had been the beginning of my journey.

Life was full of disappointments, but only when we learned to balance our losses and gains did we learn to succeed. I had lost a lot, but what I'd gained that day on the deck of the boat while coming to New York was a treasure, and I believed I deserve to be loved, cared for, looked after, and appreciated. That was what I'd found with Lady after I lost it all. I'd found a home away from home, love away from home, and success away from home, but would I find total happiness? I guessed it was up to me and how much I learned from every person around me.

I had to allow my past to be a memory and keep it as one of the stories I would tell my children. Things were getting more serious with Robert, and I knew that soon he would propose. Was I ready to say, "I do"? Would I ever be ready to pause the past where it let go of me? They were questions I feared facing; therefore, I told Robert I needed to see Julia during my next trip to his parents'.

Shortly after, it was time for Angela to graduate. Time flew by fast, and we received an official invitation to attend, with a dinner invitation at the embassy right after. Ronald told me he was planning to officially propose to Angela during the dinner ceremony. I went with him to choose the beautiful ring he got her. I was in charge of the catering, of course, but mainly, I was planning the event with him. Lady, Robert, and I met on many occasions to plan the news for her parents, especially because we knew that her dad was coming the day of the graduation. We used our connections through the embassy, and Robert,

Lady, and Ronald went to meet Angela's parents in Europe before they reached the States. Ronald was determined to have their consent in order for Angela to move into her future smoothly. It was a gentlemanly decision, and I valued him for that. All three of them flew the next day. We kept Angela in the dark with our fingers crossed, hoping for positive news. Their trip was short, and within five days, they came back to the graduation. Angela was anxious, especially since her dad was attending, but I could not tell her about the news, because I did not know how the father would take the news, and I wanted to keep the proposal a surprise.

The graduation day came. We were all ready, anxious, and waiting impatiently. Many details I did not know, but I heard it was a positive trip. After all, what would a dad want other than the happiness of his daughter?

We started at the university. Unfortunately, the flight of Angela's parents was delayed, so they did not attend the graduation. It was less stressful for her, and afterward, they were at the embassy, waiting for all of us. The stress she felt was intense. I told her, "Trust yourself, trust Ronald, and trust God. It is your night. Be happy."

When we got to the embassy, many of Ronald's friends were there. His parents surprised us, and of course, Angela's parents were there as well. She was nervous about seeing all of them and having them under one roof, but Ronald, Robert, and Lady had prepared everyone. When Angela arrived, everyone started clapping for her, and they flew congratulation balloons up in the air. When she saw all of them there drinking and laughing, she felt comfortable and loosened up. Dinner was served, and toasts were made to a great future. After dinner, everyone moved to the garden to the sound of the saxophone. The stars glowed brightly in the skies as everyone walked around, and then it was time for the big surprise. Despite the reassurances I'd heard from Robert and Lady, I was still worried, but I hoped for the best.

The lights went off, except one spot in the middle, with an alley of candles lit on both sides. At the end of the alley stood Angela, wearing a beautiful silver dress. Ronald went to the podium and took the microphone. Angela's heart started beating faster, and he asked for everyone's attention.

"Today is a very special night," he said, "not only because the stars are glowing so brightly but because the universe brought together loved ones. I would like to welcome Angela's parents and mine and take the opportunity to ask Angela's dad for his consent to unite our future."

Angela thought it was a political conciliation; she was too nervous to understand.

"With my blessings," her father said.

Then Ronald knelt on one knee. "Angela, my love, will you accept my hand in marriage?"

She was shocked and burst into tears. Her dad came to her and told her, "Any man who crosses the continent for my consent is a gentleman worth having my blessings." He held her hand and walked her to Ronald. "Let this day be the beginning of a great union," he told them.

Ronald stood, put the ring on Angela's finger, and carried her around, and they opened the dance floor.

If love is not the healer of all, what else would heal years of conflicts? It was a fairy tale and well deserved. I was happy for Angela. Everyone was dancing. Robert and I were as well, when he said, "I love you, my Ale."

Robert had expressed his love many times, but this time, it was different. "I want us to have a vacation," he said. "You deserve a break. You have been working very hard. Where would you like to go?"

I looked at him and said, "I would like to see Julia first together. Then we'll go on the boat for a couple of days."

"It shall be," he said while kissing my forehead and then the side of my lips. He followed with a special, passionate kiss.

The evening ended successfully. Everyone was happy, and Angela's happiness was beyond description. I was happy for Angela; finally, she had united with her love and with both fathers' consent. But all I could think was *Will it ever happen to me?*

We moved back to the hotel, where Lady took care of the accommodations for both sets of parents and their guests. Champagne was served on the rooftop, and we all went up. It was a cozy evening that brought the families closer together. It seemed they got to know each other all over again. It was sad how years were lost over conflicts caused by external factors and how people's lives changed as they lived miles apart from their hometowns and each other. *It is sad. Why can't things just be solved peacefully?*

Shortly, Angela's mom came to me and said, "I want to thank you for embracing my daughter at a time when she felt rejected by her own family. You, Lady, and this gentleman standing by you. I hope to see you next in line; you deserve to be happy, my sweet daughter, if you'll allow me to call you so. Any family that welcomes my daughter becomes hers and then mine. When is your big day, my dear?" she asked.

I turned red and speechless. Lady saved the moment from the question I was avoiding and said, "She is in good hands, and in due time, it will happen."

Robert put his arm around my shoulders and, not letting

the moment pass vainly, answered, "Ale deserves the best. I am standing by her today, tomorrow, and forever, but she is too precious to move into a new step without those she deserves around her."

I looked at him and wanted to thank him thoroughly for not letting me feel unworthy, and I guessed he understood my look.

The next morning, we flew to upstate New York. Robert and I both went to see Julia. The environment was so comfortable that I even forgot Julia's old story with Robert. I guessed men played a huge role in reassuring their woman of their loyalty, and Robert was a master in doing so. We sat there, and for the next forty minutes, all I could talk about was the happiness taking place around me, including the developments with Georgia, Andrew, and Angela. I was not focused; I jumped from one story to the other, talking nonstop, as if I had a lot to say with little time. The many emotional moments of those I loved were bringing my memories to the surface. After forty minutes, I paused.

"Are you happy?" Julia said.

Without hesitance, I answered, "What is not to be happy about?" while looking at Robert. My answer was from the heart, for truly, I was happy and blessed.

"Are you proud of yourself?" Julia said.

"Of course," I answered. "I'm a small-town girl using all the stones that stood in her way to build stairs to a higher level in order to reach her dream."

"Are you thinking about your parents?" Julia said.

"I can't stop thinking about them. I have been putting myself in every situation around me while living their life and mine through them. It has been very difficult."

"What have you been thinking?" asked Julia. "Can you specify the ideas?"

"Too many," I said. "I cannot separate anger from deception. I cannot identify shame from disappointment from rejection. Is it normal, after all these years, to wonder about the past? And in addition to all, I cannot stop thinking about Alisa, but is she wondering about me?"

"Alexandra, my dear," said Julia, "at a specific point in life, you have to stop and unload the past. I know your first reaction will be 'The past is not delaying me,' and it is obvious via your success, but as well it is obvious that your personal life was set aside without clarifications, and you have unanswered questions from your parents. I believe you viewed the change in lifestyle of those around you, and you started thinking about your own and not on a professional level, in addition to the closeness you are feeling with Robert. Honestly, I am not worried about the love you have for each other, but I am very concerned about you moving on into the future while held back with questions in the past."

Robert intervened. "Let us go visit your parents. Let us open a new page. I believe it is time to unload."

"Thank you, Julia," I said.

Robert and I spent the next few days on the yacht, relaxing and discussing our next trip. I was anxious and worried about their reaction, wondering how much I needed to tell them beyond my professional development. Should I start with Alex and then move on to Alisa, or should I limit things to the present? I had no answers, and moreover, Robert wanted me to relax and not plan any conversation; he just wanted me to follow my instincts and go with the flow.

"They might shock you," he said. "Just be my Ale, and let things be."

"After our return, I would like to find Alisa and make sure she is happy," I said.

"I told you I am waiting for your signal," Robert answered with a smile.

We decided to travel in two days. I informed Lady, and she offered to join. Robert welcomed her suggestion, and of course, I did too.

We left on the trip. I was silent throughout. It felt as if it were my last destination. I was so anxious that I could not remember the past. Would they be surprised to see me? Would they be happy to see me?

Robert squeezed my hand and said, "It will all be fine. We will be landing in ten minutes."

Between the airport and Farmville was forty minutes' drive. I felt my heart stopping. "Ale," said Robert, "listen to me. You survived on your own. You are only here to unload the past. Remember, you are not here for their consent, yet I am positive they will be thrilled to see you."

"Oh, look—Alisa's products are in town," I said. "Robert, did you?"

"Of course, my dear," said Robert. "There is no better place to launch a product than through its hometown!"

My tears started dropping from joy; I couldn't help it. Then Lady said, "It looks like a blessed trip so far."

We reached Farmville. I almost did not recognize my own hometown. Except for the greenery surrounding the house on the hill, my own home, everything else had changed. I felt numb, without any feelings at all.

Lady said, "Ale, give your dad some time. He may not recognize you directly."

I looked at her to answer, but I heard my brothers'

voices yelling while they ran toward me. With hugs and kisses, they took me inside the house. My mom could not stand under the shock of the surprise. She opened her arms wide, and I knelt on the floor near her, hugging her.

Then I felt a wheelchair behind me. "Do we have guests?" said my dad.

I stood in front of him, but he did not recognize me. My mom held my hand tightly. "Alzheimer's," she said.

"Your daughter," I said to him.

"Yes, I know," he answered. I smiled, thinking he recognized me, and Robert squeezed my hand. Then my father said, "I will call my daughter. She is in there. Ale!" He called out loudly. "That is my daughter. Do you know her? Her name is Alexandra."

A young lady came out. "It's fine, Grandpa," she said. "You can call me whatever you want." She looked at me and said, "My name is Alisa. Nice meeting you!"

CHAPTER TWENTY ONE

Someone please wake me up. Please. The dream is too beautiful to be a reality. What happened? What did I miss?

I was talking, but the words were not heard; my voice was muted.

"This is Alisa," Robert said.

I couldn't stand anymore. I sat on the floor near my mom. I was there to see my parents, but I forgot all about them.

Everyone was silent but Alisa. "Yes, I am Alisa," she said. "Lady and Robert told me all about you, and I couldn't wait for this day to come."

"Yes, I am your mommy, and I am sorry it took me so long to come see you," I said.

"I received all your letters and your gifts, but I always hoped for this day," Alisa said. She sat near me on the floor, wrapped her arms around me, and said, "I am still wearing the necklace you put around my neck when I was a baby, and every night, I looked at the imprint and said, 'I love you too,' and hoped you would hear me."

"I did, my Alisa. I will never let go of you again," I said.

It was an emotional evening full of tears and joy. My dad was in his own world, and sadly, he did not recognize me, but I was glad he thought I was near him through Alisa. My mom had aged, but she was still healthy, thanks to Lady, who kept them busy with Alisa and took care of all their financial needs.

Mom prepared dinner, and my whole family gathered around. During dinner, as we were toasting to our reunion, there was a knock on the door. I went to get the door, and there stood a delivery boy with one flower and a box. "Looking for Alexandra," he said.

"I am Alexandra."

"Can you please sign the receipt for the package?"

I did, and then I went back to the table where we were gathered. Everyone was looking at me, waiting for me to read the card.

I held the envelope with shaking hands. I opened it and read: "Ale, my love, you are as unique as this flower, and inside the box you will find my lifelong commitment to you."

Robert looked at me and said, "I was waiting for this moment, for all your family to be around, to ask for this commitment." He asked me to open the box, and as I did, he knelt on the floor in front of me and added, "Will you

CHAPTER TWENTY ONE

Someone please wake me up. Please. The dream is too beautiful to be a reality. What happened? What did I miss?

I was talking, but the words were not heard; my voice was muted.

"This is Alisa," Robert said.

I couldn't stand anymore. I sat on the floor near my mom. I was there to see my parents, but I forgot all about them.

Everyone was silent but Alisa. "Yes, I am Alisa," she said. "Lady and Robert told me all about you, and I couldn't wait for this day to come."

"Yes, I am your mommy, and I am sorry it took me so long to come see you," I said.

"I received all your letters and your gifts, but I always hoped for this day," Alisa said. She sat near me on the floor, wrapped her arms around me, and said, "I am still wearing the necklace you put around my neck when I was a baby, and every night, I looked at the imprint and said, 'I love you too,' and hoped you would hear me."

"I did, my Alisa. I will never let go of you again," I said.

It was an emotional evening full of tears and joy. My dad was in his own world, and sadly, he did not recognize me, but I was glad he thought I was near him through Alisa. My mom had aged, but she was still healthy, thanks to Lady, who kept them busy with Alisa and took care of all their financial needs.

Mom prepared dinner, and my whole family gathered around. During dinner, as we were toasting to our reunion, there was a knock on the door. I went to get the door, and there stood a delivery boy with one flower and a box. "Looking for Alexandra," he said.

"I am Alexandra."

"Can you please sign the receipt for the package?"

I did, and then I went back to the table where we were gathered. Everyone was looking at me, waiting for me to read the card.

I held the envelope with shaking hands. I opened it and read: "Ale, my love, you are as unique as this flower, and inside the box you will find my lifelong commitment to you."

Robert looked at me and said, "I was waiting for this moment, for all your family to be around, to ask for this commitment." He asked me to open the box, and as I did, he knelt on the floor in front of me and added, "Will you accept me as your life partner, your lover, and the man by your side?"

"I do," I said. Inside the box was a ring, along with a key with an inscription—the key to our future together.

Mine was a story worth writing, a happy ending, a fairy tale, a love story. It was the story of a woman who took a detour—in fact, many of them.

My story was not unique, nor was Lady's, Georgia's, or Angela's. Sometimes, while growing, we found ourselves standing at a crossroad. Sometimes we needed time alone, time to grow, time to develop, and space to spread our wings. Other times, we just accepted what we were given and went with the flow.

If you believe in fate and believe that your life is a drawn path, you cannot take any step beyond it. In this case, you are a person with classic beliefs, one who cannot cross any path. When faced with crossroads, you will just go back where you left off, pick up the ashes of the past, and accept what you were born to live. But if you believe in fate and believe that you are in charge of your own destiny and your own dream, then you can take charge of your life and become the master of your own destiny.

Lady made her own destiny; she let go of her love to build her future. Angela united with the love she believed in and mastered her own destiny through the peace group she had launched back in Africa. Georgia never remarried, and she became a speaker for the battered and abused. As for me, I had a happy ending and was the master of my life alongside an endless love and a great man.

I took a detour, but what if? When my parents gave

me the choice that night to leave or stay, what if I had chosen to stay? What if I had never met Lady on the boat to the big city that night? What if? Life is a combination of challenges; it is up to us to accept, ignore, or delete them.

Women who take detours in life never know where those detours might take them. Some detours lead to more pain, and others lead to happiness, but I believe when we have the will to succeed, God will join hands with us to reach our destiny.

I believe if we ask, God will listen.

I believe if we dare, we will succeed.

I believe we are faced with crossroads for a reason; they are part of the original plan.

I believe that fate and destiny will unite for us to reach our dreams.

As a small-town girl who took a detour and faced every challenge, I tell you, my friends, dare to dream. After all, dreams are part of reality!

ABOUT THE AUTHOR

Badiaa Hiresh was born in 1964 in Lebanon, where she lived and worked, raising two daughters. She also lived in the United States, which gave her an international perspective on her home country. She has worked in the family jewelry business and in education and encourages women to speak through her blog, *Your Everyday Coffee*. Hiresh is also the author of *Mommy, I Am a Pacer* and *Where Is My Angel?*

CPSIA information can be obtained
at www.ICGtesting.com
Printed in the USA
BVHW082057210921
617192BV00004B/416